TASSO'S JOURNEY

For Soula

Tasso's JOURNEY

A NOVEL

Paula Renee Burzawa

Always Have Faith!

Paula Burzawa

iUniverse®

TASSO'S JOURNEY
A NOVEL

iUniverse books may be ordered through booksellers or by contacting:

iUniverse
1663 Liberty Drive
Bloomington, IN 47403
www.iuniverse.com
1-800-Authors (1-800-288-4677)

ISBN: 978-1-4917-5538-9 (sc)
ISBN: 978-1-4917-5539-6 (hc)
ISBN: 978-1-4917-5537-2 (e)

Library of Congress Control Number: 2015901267

Printed in the United States of America.

iUniverse rev. date: 2/2/2015

This is a work of fiction. All characters, names, incidents, organizations, and dialogue in this novel either are products of the author's imagination or are used fictitiously.

For my maternal grandfather, Anastasios Stamatopoulos (Tasso), and his adoring family: my Yiayia Diamanto, Aunt Elaine, and Uncle George and my beautiful mother, Maria.

Heartfelt gratitude is extended to my mother, Uncle Nikola, Uncle Danny, Yiani, Katherine, Maggie, and Jim Shepard along with his amazing group at Sirenland 2013. Only with your contributions could I piece together this historical tale of an incredible man during an extraordinary time.

To my family with love.

Past the kitchen stood a small tool room with a door that led out to the abandoned chicken coop. I liked to go back there every now and then and look at the decaying building, still untouched from the time my mother's father, Anastasios, was alive. I imagined him inside the tiny, white-stoned structure, collecting chicken eggs from the chickens and bringing his yield to Yiayia. For some reason, I felt his presence there more than anywhere else in our Magoula home. The chicken coop was the only edifice left alone since his death. Standing near the tattered, old shack was the closest I could feel to a man I never knew, in a place he left long ago.

—Paula Renee Burzawa, *Seasons of Sun*

CONTENTS

Chapter One

A steady stream of blood trickled across the bruised knuckles that grasped all he owned. Only an empty canteen, a wool cap, a left glove, and a treasured letter from Diamanto remained in the bag he pulled desperately over his bruised shoulder. His bread was gone, and so was his pocketknife, stolen by the enemy. With a badly injured knee bleeding through dirty bandages, Tasso limped slowly along the narrow path through the dry brush.

The sun was about to set, and Tasso knew the blaring summer heat would diminish during the darkened hours. Grateful to have already crossed Corinth, he headed onward toward Parnonas as daytime faded. With less than an hour of light and the absence of an abundant moon, Tasso stopped to examine the breaks in the hillsides ahead. Where was he? He wasn't exactly sure, but he knew it best to stop as evening approached and wait until morning to continue, when he could navigate through the mountains, correctly directing himself through the Peloponnese, toward home.

This was the twelfth day he had walked without seeing a soul. Most of the women and children had already hidden deep in their villages, anticipating the Nazis' arrival. Troops would be on their way after Greece's retreat from the border of Albania, and now the race was on between the oppressor and the oppressed. The enemy would spread like ants through his country. They would kill and steal whatever they wished. He had never seen such heartlessness, the devil in their eyes. What few soldiers remained were in a pathetic race for their lives, painstakingly attempting to reach hometowns and prepare for occupation. He had not seen any of his compatriots, who had spread in all directions, since the retreat. Tasso gathered that many of them were already dead, having succumbed to the rugged mountains with no food or water, a far worse death than being killed in battle. How he had survived almost two days since his rations expired was beyond understanding. Left with only his will to reach another town and beg for food, Tasso knew his chances for survival were slim. *How many of us remain?* he silently asked the vanishing, amber sun as its deepening light disappeared behind the mountains.

Unable to decipher the shadows ahead, he paused under a large, aged olive tree to rest. Making sure to remain far from the road, he pulled his wool cap from his satchel and laid his head down on a stone. As soon as he closed his eyes, the sound of gunfire returned to his mind, which was ever haunted by images of bloodshed. *They fought so hard*, he thought. So many young men gone. How could he dispel the images after witnessing so many of his comrades killed? The enemy was too strong, like a vicious wolf fighting a wounded dog. Only weeks into their defensive attempts, the Greeks had called retreat, and the last effort to defend what remained had begun.

Opening his eyes to dispel the memories of war, he gazed at the majestic Mediterranean sky; its thick, indigo carpeting appeared bedazzled with diamonds. Each star called out to his heart. Their bright, crystal voices shouted messages of hope and love. *Get home*, the magical sky entreated his soul. *Get home*. The little one would be walking by now, and George and Elaine would be running circles around Diamanto's skirts, asking for food.

"Lord, let them be healthy," he prayed as his large raven eyes fogged with tears. Stretching his long body across the brush, he strained to cover his limbs with what dried grasses he could find on the hard, thorny ground. Forcing his mind to focus on more comforting images of his wife, Tasso tried to drift off for the night but not before the memory of her words took over his last thought: Diamanto's plea that he not fight, an entreaty that had turned resentful, repeated in his mind.

"You put fight before family," she had told him the morning he departed, even though only the lame and old remained behind. Tasso did his best to appease his young wife, but his efforts were lost to the anger that rose in her eyes. "You choose *this*?" she had asked him. Denying his own reservations, even to himself, Tasso had hoped to convince her he was unrelenting in his decision. Now he heard her stinging statement repeatedly in his dreams.

The sun woke him hours later. Grateful the night had passed without disruption, he sat up and was instantly reminded of his pain. A tingling sensation like small daggers spread across his cut knee, but there was no time to worry about his wounds. A third day without water would be his demise. Finding nourishment was his only hope. He reexamined his injured leg, still a rainbow of colors from the dried blood and infection that had set into the skin. Unable to stand on his first or second try, Tasso stopped for a moment and steadied himself on his good knee, before attempting to pull his body up, bracing against a large olive tree.

Please, Lord, he prayed silently, too weak to speak aloud as he knelt, *let me find water today. Let me get home. Please, Lord, save my family.*

Anchoring his right arm over the break in the tree trunk, Tasso hoisted his torso up with all his strength, setting his good leg down first and then pausing to gain balance. With difficulty, he dragged his left leg to a standing position and leaned against the tree for a moment. Looking around at his location lit by the morning's light, he knew he had to move. Increasing sweat inside his clothes from the heat was already making his cuts twinge with pain. Hunched over, he took the first steps toward the side road, watching carefully for any signs of the enemy. Slumping along, he switched hands to carry his bag and winced at his broken fingers, shuddering at the thought of not being able to hold a hammer again, unable to finish the dream house he had promised Diamanto. But he had bigger problems today, he knew—like staying alive and finding water.

Cicadas hummed around the brush, making a maddening background to this test of his sanity. With each step forward, Tasso saw Mandini's face, smiling. In his memory, he saw her smirk the first time he'd called her by that nickname. Diamanto Laskari was her full name, as he had learned the blessed day they met. But she would always be Mandini to him. Agreeing to marriage without sight of the bride was a risk for any man, but the name Laskari had been long respected for generations. Tasso, one of three brothers and a sister, had avoided the selection of a wife as long as possible. Unusually tall, with generous locks of jet-black hair, Anastasios Stamatopoulos—or Tasso, as his friends called him—stood like a giant. He could have had his pick of any young girl from neighboring villages.

But when an older cousin visited Tasso in Magoula on the way to Sparta one afternoon years ago, he became interested in the little woman named Diamanto.

"You'll like her. I promise!" the cousin pleaded as Tasso's mother stood nearby, eavesdropping.

"She's a bit older," he confessed. "Yet beautiful nonetheless."

"How old?" Tasso's mother barked, ready to quickly dispel any bad deal bestowed upon him. "He wants children, you know! Why isn't she married already? What's *wrong* with her?"

Tasso was embarrassed of her unending questions.

"Just meet her!" The eager cousin put a hand on his arm, a gentle gesture Tasso knew was meant to block out his mother's objections.

Tasso agreed, and the next day, the older cousin arranged for a secret meeting between Tasso and Diamanto. Even the girl's relatives were unaware of the rendezvous. Typically, the entire Greek family was present at such pivotal moments in a young couple's life, but Tasso was glad the old man put one over on both families, letting the two of them meet one another without the watchful eyes of others. In a grove outside Mistras, the old man said he needed Diamanto to help him pick figs in his field. Tasso was instructed to come at noon. He had been in the process of building a chicken coop for the older cousin and was coming to finish the roof.

The cousin expressed empathy for the girl whose failed previous engagement now left her unmarried well into her twenties, an unfortunate status for any young woman. Recognizing the matchmaker's attempt, Tasso saw no harm in getting a sneak preview before the negotiations between their families went any farther.

Tasso approached the field right as the sun peaked overhead, its intense heat putting the area in a blinding haze. There was a girl standing beside a fig tree with a basket on the ground next to her feet. She was pretty and very petite. He half-laughed to himself at their immense difference in stature. When he got closer, the girl put her eyes to the ground, and Tasso guessed she was waiting for a formal introduction. The older cousin must have forgotten his manners because he immediately began to boast about

Tasso's skills as a builder and craftsman, blatantly selling Tasso's attributes to the innocent, prospective bride without the expected formality.

"I'll be happy to see the project finished only if it meets your standards," Tasso said, attempting to stop the old man's rant. When he said this, the girl lifted her head. She looked at him with kind eyes and smiled, obviously taking note of the old man's poor attempt to make this encounter look accidental.

Tasso climbed a ladder and began inspecting the roof, uneasily waiting for an introduction.

The girl stayed by the tree, busily picking figs, until finally the old man called out, "Oh my! Forgive me, sweetheart—I've been so improper! Come meet Tasso, my younger cousin from Magoula. His father was my mother's second cousin from Astros. We spent summers together in Sparta years ago."

Tasso climbed down from the ladder and wiped his hands on a rag from his back pocket.

"Tasso, may I introduce you to Diamanto Laskari of Vassara, daughter of Kotso and Georgia." The old man turned to the girl. "Diamanto, this is Anastasios Stamatopoulos of Magoula, Sparta."

"Pleased to meet you. Please call me Tasso." He smiled as Diamanto returned his look and nodded, stretching a wide grin. He liked her instantly.

Their exchanges were few but polite for the next hour or so, until the old man stepped away to water his donkey, another matchmaker's trick to give them privacy. When the old man didn't return after a few minutes, Tasso became worried and left Diamanto alone to look for him. Returning to her laughing, he informed Diamanto that her chaperone for the afternoon had fallen asleep in the shade. He suggested they too move out of the sun and share the lunch the cousin prepared for them that was tied up in satchels inside the old man's cart. He was eager to have time alone with the pretty girl from Vassara.

They stretched out a cloth under an olive tree nearby, in a spot that was shaded but close enough to the cart and the old man. Diamanto spread out the kasseri and feta cheeses, bread, tomatoes, and melon.

"Would you care for something?" Diamanto held out a piece of bread to Tasso.

"After you," Tasso insisted.

She smiled and looked downward, obviously trying to hide her grin.

Tasso could sense the girl was nervous, so he tried to put her at ease. "I'm told you are also from Vassara. Is the village as beautiful as people say?"

"Vassara is the *most* beautiful. Perhaps not as exciting as a city like Sparta but breathtaking in its views of Parnonas." When she talked about her birthplace, Diamanto seemed to relax. Tasso let her continue describing her hometown in great detail. He could only stare at her beauty. Diamanto's demeanor was that of a blissful yet humble girl. When she smiled, the shine in her eyes made him calm and happy.

"Vassara sounds incredible. Perhaps I can visit someday," he suggested.

"That would be nice." She blushed and then laughed.

Regardless of her petite frame, she seemed to be a giant in warmth and honesty. He didn't care about her age. In fact, twenty-three quite suited him for a bride because she was still younger than his twenty-eight. The broken arrangement from her past betrothal was his gain now.

Then she surprised him by saying, "You know, I'm not the *youngest* of girls from Vassara. There are others much more suited in age for marriage."

Pleased by her openness, he replied, "Suited in age perhaps but not for me. Your uncle told me of your broken betrothal. I regret your misfortune." There was a momentary silence. "You were fond of him?" he continued, looking directly into her eyes.

"I didn't know him," she said. "He was the son of my uncle's friend."

Tasso exhaled, relieved to know she wasn't harboring old feelings for another man.

Surprisingly, Diamanto offered more. "When the dowry failed to arrive in time from my older sister in America, his parents broke the engagement." She paused again. "I was told the boy asked for the marriage to proceed even without the money, but his parents refused."

Tasso, imagining his own mother's strict expectations, related to the boy's predicament. "God has a way of bestowing many blessings on us throughout our lives. I believe great things await you." He placed his large hand over hers.

When the old man woke up, he joined the pair as they finished the homemade wine. Tasso's cousin appeared content with his successful scheme. Likewise, Tasso felt a warm glow of happiness running through his body. The rest would be easy, he thought as he put his arm around his cousin, giving a tight squeeze of appreciation as they prepared to part ways.

"Thank you for working on the roof, Tasso. I knew your talents would not disappoint me."

"I thank *you*," said Tasso. "This is sure to be the highlight of my day." He looked straight at Diamanto as he spoke. She beamed at him.

"It would be my pleasure to see you again, Miss Laskari." He tried to memorize the details of her face. When their cart trotted away, there was a pull at his heart, one that would return every time he and his Mandini parted thereafter.

Recollections of their first meeting fed his soul with the happiness of a simpler time. Yet his physical body could not continue. As he thought again of his wife's hardened words, the pain of guilt returned. He had been torn between his love for family and obligation to country, and he surmised he had failed both. *With me left to die like this*, he thought, *she will never know my regrets, never understand my misgivings. I have made a difference to no one.*

He trudged along the dirt path, disoriented by dehydration, his wounded leg almost too heavy to drag. Stumbling on the root of a tree he did not notice, Tasso fell hard on the ground, reopening the wound on his head. He felt his body go limp and anticipated losing consciousness. He closed his eyes in resignation while cicadas disturbed the silence.

With an abrupt inhaled breath, Tasso gasped. His head pounded with pain. There was blood where he lay. How long had he been out? Trying to reassess his situation, he slowly sat up. Then his heart jumped at a sound—like trickles at first, but then undeniable. He heard water. Tasso turned his body and listened more. As the sound grew, he wearily managed to stand and stumble along toward the unquestionable sound, to his salvation: a river!

With an audible moan of joy, Tasso collapsed his weakened body at the edge and splashed the cool wetness about his face. Cupping his broken hands, he brought water to his dry, cracked mouth and felt the relief go down his throat and through his body. He lay there, repeatedly bringing water to his mouth. He could not get enough. In a semiconscious state, he was about to drift off again when he heard an animal cry out.

Looking up, he saw a small gray donkey standing about twenty feet from him, drinking from the riverbank. A long, bristled rope hung around its thick neck, tailing behind and resting on the ground. This animal belonged to someone. *People!* thought Tasso, as he prayed a band of Germans hadn't stolen livestock from a village. Unable to rise to his feet with speed, he slid along the side of the river, trying not to startle the animal. Looking around, the wounded veteran saw no sign of the enemy, no trucks on the road. If the animal were stolen, surely there would be more creatures or vehicles. Looking for a place to hide, he hoped the donkey would not call attention to him.

Chapter Two

"There you are!" Tasso heard someone shout. He looked up and saw a short old man limping over to the donkey. The man held out a hand to reach for the rope that trailed from the donkey's neck. Wrapping the rope around his wrist several times, the old man touched the donkey's side, stroking the animal.

"My dear one, you are more parched than I thought. Come now! You can't be *that* thirsty. We haven't been gone that long." Tasso watched as the man spoke to his donkey while letting it suck in more water. He tried to cry out as the old man had his eyes focused on the animal, but no sound came out. He struggled to lift an arm, but his lifeless body would not cooperate.

The old man looked up at the sun and wiped his forehead with a kerchief from his pocket. "That's enough. Time to head toward the other field. And after that, our lunch awaits us back home. Remember?"

The animal snorted loudly.

Tasso knew any attempt to mutter a weakened call for help would be overpowered by the donkey's cries, but he tried anyway. He pushed his torso upward, but his body fell back to the ground with a thump.

The old man turned his head. "Mother of God!" he exclaimed. "Christo! Come quick!"

A second old man appeared with another donkey tethered to a long leather strap. "Oh my Lord, a soldier!" he exclaimed. Both men knelt down at his body. Tasso's head was quickly propped up on one man's lap while the other cupped cold water onto his face. Tasso opened his lips to let the water trickle in.

"Where did he come from?"

"I have no idea, but keep his head up, Christo. I will go and get my satchel. This poor soul is barely alive."

Tasso listened to the men talk but couldn't answer.

The old man returned carrying a white cotton bundle. He placed it on the ground and unwrapped a dark half-loaf of bread. They looked at him with concern while the first man broke off a small piece and dipped it in the river. When a small, saturated piece was held to his face, Tasso's lips trembled to open. He tried to speak but could only nod.

"Save your strength," the old man said.

Tasso slowly pointed to his bad leg through the rip in his pants.

The old man nodded to his friend, saying, "Christo, we have to get him to the village. This leg is bad." Then he turned to Tasso again and said, "I am Niko." He placed his open palm on Tasso's chest. "My friend Christo and I will help you. We are from Elaiohori, nearby."

Christo got up and brought the second donkey toward Tasso. After giving him more bread and water, the old men gently hoisted his body atop their animal with difficulty. Pain shot throughout his body as they awkwardly lifted his injured limbs. Barely able to balance, he rested his torso on the animal's neck. The old men gathered their satchels and walked slowly, leading the donkey that carried him. He was barely awake and fought hard to keep his eyes open while resting atop the donkey.

"My home is just around the bend of this hill," Niko said. He turned with a grin toward him, a look of relief on his wrinkled, aged face—that of a shepherd, Tasso guessed. As they turned around the hill, village homes came into view, spread across the mountain.

"We are almost here!" the old man said. "My wife Antonia will give you food. Christo and I can fetch a man to look at your wounds. We will take care of you."

Hearing her husband's call from the road, Antonia immediately knew something was off. In the forty-two years they had been married, Niko and his friend had gone out together daily, and unless the weather turned inclement, she never remembered them returning so soon. Coming to her low-framed kitchen door, she squinted at the sunshine and saw the two approaching with what appeared to be a third man, his body slumped over the donkey's neck. He looked unconscious. She hurried to start a fire for hot water.

Antonia called to her eldest grandson. The six-year-old in torn shorts with thick black curls covering his forehead came running from the bedroom.

"Fetch Mr. Spiropoulos right away!" she told him, retying the stained apron that covered her blue housedress.

"What's wrong, Yiayia? Is someone hurt?" the child asked as he headed for the door.

"Yes. Tell him to come at once! Go! Go!"

"Yes, Yiayia!" The boy dashed off in an instant, up the main road toward the square.

Antonia helped her husband and Niko lift the stranger and stretch his body across two benches inside their courtyard. She prepared warm wet cloths to clean him. Not long after, Mr. Spiropoulos, the town physician, arrived and began to inspect the man.

Shaking his head, he said, "Good thing you found this poor soul, Niko. He wouldn't have lasted much longer. He is quite dehydrated, and this leg is bad. He should not be moved for a while. The infection needs to be cleaned."

"T-a-a-s ..." the man uttered.

Antonia jumped when the stranger tried to speak. "What did he say?" She bent down to hear.

"M-m-my name is Tasso," he said weakly.

Niko handed her another clean, warm cloth, which she held to the soldier's forehead. "We will care for you," she said comfortingly. Tears streamed down her cheeks as she patted his face with the cloth. She looked up at the men and saw Christo wipe back a tear as well.

The four stripped away Tasso's tattered clothing, hardened by dirt and blood. Antonia winced as the soldier cried out despite their slow, gentle movements. As each article was removed, a different injury was revealed. Mr. Spiropoulos used various ointments from his bag, and the soldier flinched at every application. She felt sorry for him and had to turn her face away several times.

They spent over an hour washing him from head to foot. A foul stench filled the air during the painstakingly slow task. Antonia placed a small bowl on a stool to wash the blood out of the soldier's hair. Thankfully, his scalp was free of lice, she thought. Finally, she assisted the physician in disinfecting a gash on his forehead. The doctor showed her how the cuts had been stitched skillfully.

"Perhaps he was in an army hospital of some sort," she suggested.

"That's my assumption," Mr. Spiropoulos agreed. "He appears to have already obtained medical care. Otherwise, these injuries would be much worse." He paused and then added, "The leg, however, is a problem. He must not try to walk on it."

Antonia nodded, thinking of how he could rest in her son's vacant room while she tended to his needs. Then she began what would be several trips to the back of the house carrying dirtied shreds of his garments.

Behind her kitchen sat a large pot filled with boiling water that she had prepared. While adding the garments to the pot, she reminded herself to keep her composure. She could cry later. She was placing Tasso's clothing in the boiling water to sterilize anything that might be salvaged. Using a large wooden stick, Antonia pressed the clothing below the surface of the heated water. She stirred the items, doubting anything would be useful again.

Reaching for the last of his items, she found a worn satchel with several gaping holes. Inside was a photograph of a woman, one worn glove, a cap, and a dented canteen. She threw the glove and hat into the pot as well and examined the photo, noticing the young woman's sweet smile. She put the picture in her apron pocket. Coming back into the courtyard, Antonia saw Mr. Spiropoulos, Niko, and Christo hoisting the soldier's body into the front room of her house toward her son's empty bedroom. She ran ahead to turn the sheets down, arriving just in time to place a small pillow underneath his head. "Thank you," the soldier muttered as the three older men situated his body across the bed that barely accommodated his large frame. Antonia looked at the soldier now clothed in her son's shirt and pants, the latter rolled up to the knee, exposing his leg injuries.

Christo said, "To think how tall your son is, Niko, and still his trousers aren't long enough!"

Antonia leaned over to observe the wrappings Mr. Spiropoulos had created for the wound. Seeing the soldier wearing her son's garments was difficult. The soldier reached for her hands and grasped them together inside of his palms. Thinking of her own son, she fought hard to fashion a brave smile for her new guest. Reaching into her pocket, she pulled out the photo and placed it in his hands. He looked down and closed the picture tight within his palms. A tear streamed out the side of his eye. Antonia nodded to him, with tears of her own trailing down her wrinkled cheeks.

That night and for several nights thereafter, she sat sleeplessly at the young man's side, monitoring fever, bleeding, and dehydration. Once he had enough to eat and drink, his health gradually returned. Although his head wounds improved every day, his leg remained a problem. Antonia was impressed with the speed of his recovery and came to the opinion that he was stronger than most men, both in his body and in his mind. Two weeks after he was found, the soldier, now nourished and well rested, was able to sit up and speak with ease.

Tasso turned to her one day when she brought fresh water to his bedside. "I can't thank you enough for your kindness, Mrs. Pappaioannou," he said.

"You must call me Antonia, Tasso. You've been in my house too long to be so formal!" She laughed as Tasso rested his head back on the pillow behind him and grinned. Antonia glanced down at her youngest grandson. "Have you washed your hands since you were outside playing?"

"Yes, Yiayia," replied the little boy. Grigori had been sitting on the chipped wooden stool next to Tasso's bed for hours. The curious boy had stared at the soldier night and day since his arrival. Tasso patted his head with his bandaged hand.

Tasso turned to Antonia. "It's okay. I don't mind. In fact, he's just a few years younger than my son, George. Seeing your grandson is another medicine for me."

She thought of how much her grandson longed for his baba, missing since the war at the border began. Her only son, Thanasi, hadn't seen his son in two years, and Antonia wondered whether he was still alive. Nursing Tasso back to health had revealed an explosion of emotions she thought she had suppressed long ago. Unsure whether she would ever see her son again, she felt her fury over the struggles that had ripped apart her family, town, and country begin to resurface.

After everyone learned her husband and Christo had found a wounded soldier by the river, townspeople buzzed about Tasso's recovery, each of them with a different opinion. There were varied assumptions made regarding his arrival and what it might foreshadow. Although Antonia witnessed many neighbors' elation over a surviving soldier, she knew others suspected her caregiving activity since her son Thanasi was rumored to be a liberal. As part of the growing "freedom lovers" who opposed Greece's monarchy, Thanasi had joined a number of Elaiohori's young men who supported the ideas of revolutionaries like Venizelos, while others remained loyal to the king. Although they were united against an outside enemy, her town, like her country, was internally divided. As a result, curiosity grew for many reasons. She feared some called her a hypocrite behind her back. The unjustified criticism only added to her many burdens.

Antonia was certain squabbles between countrymen were capable of causing irreparable damage in her world. She did her best to avoid senseless small talk, even if that meant allowing others to judge her family incorrectly. Although conversations in the square were dominated by two topics—war with the Germans and Tasso's health—she knew darker accusations regarding her visitor were discussed. Antonia didn't care for any of it.

"His leg is getting better," the shopkeeper said as she purchased fresh loaves of bread one morning.

"He will leave us soon!" another woman announced. "He must return to the fight."

"Does he really keep a photo of King George next to his bed? I hear he is quite loyal to the king," said another old man.

"That's not what I heard!" the old woman snapped at him.

Antonia turned to them. "All we care about is his health," she told them before walking away.

As weeks progressed, Tasso got to know the people of Elaiohori. He amiably received any visitors Antonia would allow, guessing that she was not only protecting his health but protecting him from political inquiries from the townspeople as well. Elaiohori was like Vassara, he suspected—the same village in a different location. They were all alike: the shepherds, the storekeepers, the farmers, the curious old ladies, and the men left behind, too old for war but full of nostalgia. They were good people at heart, he believed, who wanted the same happy life for their children and grandchildren as everyone else. But he also knew that civil unrest had unveiled an ugly side to his countrymen, and Tasso hoped they would all unite when the war ended. He believed their differences had more to do with ignorance than anything else, since these unsuspecting people believed what they were told to believe. He felt sorry for them, isolated in their small, rural locations, away from information of the outside world.

As villagers came to meet him, many brought gifts of dried fruits, blankets, and handmade items. One old man brought him a wooden toy he had carved.

"I heard you have a son. This is for him," he said, showing a sculpted dog.

"You are too kind," Tasso replied.

"This is all I can do for brave men like you who delayed the enemy. The extra time helped us prepare. Some of us have even sent our daughters into hiding," the man replied with confidence. Still, other villagers kept their distance, and he assumed they had their reasons. Tasso wished they understood that he only wanted the best for all of Greece. He was generous with his time and saw as many villagers as he could, in an effort to show gratitude. He learned their names and established friendships. Some local men made him cheese and repaired his boots. Women brought cooked foods. Tasso was glad, hoping Antonia's workload might be lessened.

But in the quiet of their visits, after all well-wishes were offered, each visitor sought the same thing. Although he could tell they didn't mean to bother him, each eventually asked the same question.

"Have you seen him?" said an old man, holding a tattered, creased black-and-white photo of his uniformed son. "Does his face look familiar at all?" Tasso did his best every time, taking each photo and holding it for inspection. He felt terrible that he hadn't recognized even one. Villager after villager brought photos of missing sons, brothers, fathers, and uncles, all of them testing his memory.

"I'm so sorry. I have not," he answered time and time again, while trying to reassure the villagers that one soldier's failure to recognize these men did not say anything about whether they had survived.

One afternoon, Tasso opened his eyes and saw a young woman in his doorway, holding the hand of a toddler and carrying an infant. Antonia stood behind, her hand on the young woman's shoulder.

"That's okay, Antonia," whispered the young woman. "He sleeps still. I'll come another time."

Tasso sat up at the sight of the young mother, whose features were so similar to his beloved Mandini's. "I'm awake. Please, come in." He sat up and wiped his eyes.

"What a beautiful baby!" He smiled at the shy toddler as she hid behind her mother's skirts. The girl's big brown eyes peered out at him.

"I don't mean to bother you," said the woman. "It's just …" She began to weep, and the little girl hugged her mother's legs.

Antonia sat on the corner of the bed. "This is Margarita," Antonia explained. "Her husband Dimosteni sent a letter three months ago, but she hasn't heard from him since." The young mother appeared too emotional to speak.

Tasso held out his hand for her photo, and she passed it to him. A cold chill ran through his body as he instantly recognized the face of a gunner who had operated weaponry with him aboard their ship. Recalling the horror of seeing him killed just feet away, Tasso felt emotions explode inside of him. He took a deep breath and looked again at the innocent eyes of the little girl standing next to her mother. Careful to disguise his grief, he said, "No, I'm sorry, good woman, I do not know him." He held his breath for a minute and forced a false smile. "Have faith, though, and stay well. Mind these children for your husband, as I pray my Mandini is doing."

"Thank you," Margarita said, grinning. "May God grant you a fast recovery that you may reunite with your family soon." She left the room with Antonia's arm around her.

Tasso leaned back, closing his eyes. He felt a dagger to his heart. How could he lie? How could he tell her the truth? In one instant, he'd had the power to change this poor woman's life. He could have put her wondering to rest. But he would have broken her heart. What had he done? For a moment, he considered calling her back and confessing that he had lied to her, explaining that he hadn't had the courage to tell her he was dead. He'd beg for her forgiveness. He'd ask her to understand his predicament. What should he have done? Tasso's heart beat fast. He clenched both fists, pounding them on the mattress underneath the blanket. Damn this war! *Which pain is worse*, he asked himself, *coping with the loss of a loved one or not knowing what happened to them?* There was no choice that made sense. Like leaving his Mandini and children to defend his country, each decision brought pain, yet every choice seemed justified. He couldn't face what he had done. Suddenly, he missed his wife more than ever. Reaching for his last letter from her off the side table, Tasso brought the paper close to his chest and closed his eyes to think of her again.

A month passed, and Tasso was finally up and walking. He repaid what stewardship he could in his caretaker's home by fixing furniture, repairing cracks in the ceiling, and completing odd jobs around Niko's farm that required attention from a younger, more able body. Antonia tried to keep his activity to a minimum, insisting he save his strength for travel. Meanwhile, some of the townspeople prepared packages, to send him off with every advantage.

"A new canteen," the storekeeper said, giving him the gift when he walked through the center of town.

"Some cheeses for your journey," another man said, offering a cloth-wrapped item. Tasso expressed his heartfelt gratitude. Old women came to him with tears, saying they were sorry to see him go, but they understood he needed to be elsewhere. He feared for these generous people and for all of Greece. Anxious to return home and protect his family and knowing the journey to Vassara would take days, he wanted to begin as soon as possible.

Chapter Three

When the time came for Tasso to leave Elaiohori, Niko and Christo confessed keeping a secret. Both friends were planning to escort him home. They knew it would be dangerous, but they insisted. Tasso was touched by their offer and respected their courage, but he knew somehow he had to dispel their idea.

"We can't let you go alone," Niko told him one day as the three sat over a breakfast Antonia had prepared before going to visit Petro's wife with her grandchildren.

"Do you know what your wives will say when you tell them?" he asked.

"They'll say you are a soldier," Christo answered. "You are strong, young, and trained, and we are too old and weak to survive the journey."

Niko nodded as if he too had already planned for his wife's objections. Tasso looked down and shook his head.

Niko spoke louder. "Let them say what they want! We were once soldiers too! We know the roads. We *know* these mountains, and we know how to get you safely to the outskirts of Vassara. Surely this is of value."

Tasso turned his head to look out the kitchen window. He didn't want to offend his friends after all they had done for him. But he doubted the old men would be more of a help than a hindrance and was certain the focus of his journey would become caring about the old men's safety and not getting home as soon as possible. He wasn't sure he'd be able to put a stop to their plan, but he thanked them for their offer. To his dismay, Niko and Christo were relentless about escorting him past Elaiohori. Tasso conceded to appease them but insisted they turn back after taking him past the outskirts of their region. He estimated this wouldn't take more than a day's time.

Later that day, out by the chicken coop, Antonia tended to the chicks. The sun was about to set in a sky painted a watercolor of pink and orange. As friendship had developed between Niko and Tasso, she had presumed early on that her husband would want to take Tasso home. She dreaded the risks for her husband but knew any efforts to stop him would be a waste of time. Niko would proceed whether she approved or not. She looked up from counting chicks and found her husband of over forty years standing silently, watching her work. She said nothing. When he finally confessed his plan moments later, she hung her head and nodded. Antonia cleared her throat and asked, "When will you leave?"

"As soon as Tasso finishes the fence. He wants to change the broken latch and patch the damage from last year's storm. Most likely no longer than a day or two. Meanwhile, he's still arguing with us to let him go alone, but we know he needs us."

Antonia was distraught with worry for Niko and with the thought of bidding farewell to the stranger who had become like family.

When the rooster crowed the next morning, Tasso was already up and working. Finishing a last project, he used some old wood found in Niko's barn to mend a fence that separated animals. After laboring over an hour without breakfast, he was pleased to see Niko and Christo coming toward him with a tray.

"Do you two have coffee together *every* morning?" he laughed.

"One of the small pleasures in life," Christo answered.

"How wonderful," he answered as he turned to inspect his work. "You are more like brothers than friends, aren't you?" He thought of Dimitri, still anxious to continue the search for his brother.

"Truly," said Niko, as he handed him a cup of coffee. Tasso thanked him.

"You do amazing work!" commented Christo. He felt the fence. "You've done this work many times!"

Tasso looked down and smiled. "Actually," he said, "I started a house in Magoula."

"Magoula?" said Christo. "I thought Vassara was your home."

"It is for now. My wife was given a plot in Magoula when we got married, and we always wanted to build our perfect dream home there." He wiped his brow with a rag from his pocket and took another sip of his hot coffee, enjoying the invigorating aroma. "I'm not sure of its condition now, but the house was nearly complete when I left. We were planning to plant orange and lemon orchards."

"My goodness!" Christo replied.

Niko led them out of the sun to sit under a nearby tree. Tasso was glad to take a break. After they sat down in the shade, he looked around at the land surrounding Niko's home, surveying the property in relation to what he'd planned back home, and continued.

"I designed the house myself, leaving room for trees and a very large courtyard with a beautiful balcony. There's even a chicken coop out back. The wood for it came all the way from my parents' village of Longastra. We brought the wood down in a caravan of donkeys led by my ten-year-old nephew." He laughed. "You should have seen us." After a pause, he smiled and concluded, "Those were happy times!"

"And you have many happy years ahead of you, Tasso," Niko added. "You give that land greater value with a beautiful home. These things take time. You'll finish it."

He smiled in appreciation of the old man's confidence. "I hope so," he answered. "The orchards will be the real glory. We hope to have over 350 trees."

"That's fantastic!" said Christo.

Tasso thought he would try one more time to change their minds "So about your decision to leave …" he began.

In the end, Tasso could only shake his head, believing these stubborn old men would overcome any argument to the contrary.

The next day after sunset, Tasso watched as Niko brought three donkeys from the back of the house to the front. Fed and watered, the animals grazed in the field to prepare for the trip. Tasso had seen Antonia busily working for days, baking breads and preparing packages. After the donkeys were loaded, he spent a last quiet moment alone in the bedroom. Standing at the window, he pulled out his wife's photo once more. He was still looking at the photo of his Mandini when a noise behind him startled him.

"I'm so sorry. I didn't want to bother you," Antonia said at the door. From the look on her face, he could tell she had been crying. As he came closer, her sorrow seemed to grow into anger. He assumed she was upset about the men's plans to escort him out of Elaiohori.

"Antonia, I tried to convince them not to come."

She didn't answer but looked down at the cloth item clutched in her hands.

He added, "They promised to turn back as soon as we near Parnonas. I can't imagine that will take very long." He took a step toward her as he spoke, but when he got close, she forcefully handed him something.

"For you!" she said, shoving it at him.

He unfolded the item; it was a new satchel.

"I was sewing it for Thanasi, thinking he would come back," she said with contempt. "*You* have it." Her voice was cold.

He didn't understand at first, but then he realized she no longer expected her son to come back. "Oh, Antonia, he will return. You must have faith," he pleaded, feeling terrible that she had resigned herself to this conclusion.

He placed his arm on her shoulder, but she pushed him away and shouted, "He's not coming back!" There was a pause, and then Antonia raised her fist. "Why? Why do we have to be at odds with one another?" Her voice grew louder. "Do you know what some of the villagers are asking about *you*?"

Her comment startled him.

"They want to know what *side* you are on! Not Greek or German, but if you are loyal to the king, *unlike* my Thanasi! God only knows what will happen to him! Some of his own *Greeks* want him dead!"

Wanting to diffuse her anger, he offered, "I'm aware of the differences, Antonia, but right now we focus on one enemy."

"You don't understand!" She came at him in anger and pounded her fist on his chest. "My Thanasi isn't going to survive either way. He's *doomed*!" With that she burst into tears, burying her head in his chest.

Shocked by her outburst, he didn't know what else to do but let

Antonia pour out her angst until after several minutes she became quiet. Feeling her body shake, he advised gently, "Keep the satchel for Thanasi … and keep your faith as well."

She stepped back and asked softly, "My God, what am I doing?" She wiped her cheek with her sleeve and took the satchel he held out to her.

"He is my only son. Forgive me," she said. The room was silent for a moment before she added, "It didn't used to be like this. We used to be happy here."

Suddenly, his own sorrow emerged from an unexpected place. He couldn't hold back his own emotions, even for Antonia's sake.

"I have a brother," he said, his voice cracking. Antonia looked at him. He hadn't planned on sharing this with any of them in Elaiohori, but he needed to tell someone and felt this was the time to unload his heart as well.

"He has been missing for a long time." Tasso stopped to compose himself. "His name is Dimitri."

Antonia rested her arm on his shoulder. He was glad to spill out the details to the woman who had cared for him like a mother.

"He was with the troops in Albania, but no one has heard from him."

"Oh, Tasso!" Antonia began to cry again.

"I've been trying to learn if he is dead or alive for the longest time. I thought by now I would have found him."

"You have many burdens, don't you?" she asked, seeming ashamed.

He looked at her earnestly and took a deep breath. "We have to keep our faith, don't you see?" he said, wiping his own tear. "But as for your Thanasi, the struggles we faced in recent times tested all of our beliefs. Young men like your son have convinced themselves to turn against our government. Forgive me, Antonia, but they are ignorant and easily influenced. It's most important that we pull ourselves together so this country can survive." His look grew more sincere. "Don't give up on your son. My wife knew my brother's disappearance was on my conscience. I told her that no husband, son, or brother wants to separate from family. Whatever beliefs Thanasi has in his heart, I'm sure he cares deeply for all of you and wants to get home. There's no easy choice for us." He hoped she would understand his heartfelt words, even if they were difficult to hear.

Late into the night, Antonia turned restlessly in bed. She finally got up, lit the small oil lamp next to her bed, and quietly carried it into the kitchen so as not to disturb Niko. She peeked into the children's room, smiling at their bodies lying side by side under a blanket. With their mother deceased over a year, the absence of their father was almost more than her heart could bear. She prayed Thanasi would return like Tasso so that her grandchildren could be blessed with at least one parent. For years, Antonia's troubles had centered on her daughter-in-law's long illness and death, as well as her son's grief, but with the war, the entire world seemed to be crumbling down around her. Fear for her family's well-being was a constant emotion that never went away. She quivered with cold in the dark, silent house and placed a small pot of water near the fire to make tea. She sat alone in the kitchen, staring up at the night sky and the bright, almost full moon through the window. Closing her eyes in prayer to the Virgin Mother, Antonia asked for protection for the three men. Only with Her divine grace would they reach their destination safely. Only with God's infinite blessings would her family reunite in a time of peace. Would they be so blessed? As she crossed herself, she heard shuffling from down the hall. Tasso was awake. It was time.

"Did I disturb you?" she asked him.

"No. I was awake," he answered. "Too anxious, I suppose. Far too many thoughts on my mind." He sat at the table and added, "Words can never express the gratitude I feel in my heart for you and your family. I would be dead if your husband and Christo hadn't found me by the river. Thank you, Antonia. Thank you for saving me."

"May you go with God," she said as Niko shuffled into the room, his eyes half-closed.

"It is time?" he asked wearily.

"Yes," replied Tasso.

"Your tea is ready," she interjected, beginning to move with purpose in the kitchen, eager to fulfill the men's needs. She wanted to make sure they all left with full stomachs. Not long after, there was a muffled rap at the door.

"Good morning, Christo!" Tasso said, greeting the older gentleman.

"I'm not sure what it is—morning or night. What time is it anyway?" he asked as he sat down.

"Time to leave," Niko replied.

Antonia could tell her husband was anxious. "Have you finished your food, Tasso? Niko, let the man eat," she retorted, hoping to delay their exit.

"I'm fine. Niko is right. We should get started," Tasso answered, drinking a last sip of tea. The three men rose from the table.

Antonia kissed Christo on both cheeks and then Tasso. "May we see each other again," she said softly. Christo and Tasso headed out the door as Niko walked slowly over to her. She started to tear up, despite her best efforts.

"We will be fine. I will see you soon, my love. Be brave. Mr. Spiropoulos will check in every day as I have asked of him. Should you need anything …"

She interrupted her husband. "Niko, please, my love, be careful. You are not as young as you think." He kissed her softly and headed out the door where the donkeys were tied. She looked on as Tasso and Christo stood next to the animals, preparing to bring them down to the main road.

Soon the three men were distant figures in the waning moonlight. Antonia watched their shadows move in unison, with shining stars stretching like a garland over their heads. The moon faded as the evening reached its final hours. She stood alone in the doorway, leaning against the cold stone wall of her home, staring at their silhouettes until she could no longer make out their forms. Like the three wise men, she thought as she crossed herself, they traveled by the light of the moon to reach their destiny. She prayed they would be safe.

Chapter Four

To Tasso's surprise, Niko and Christo kept a quick pace. He tried to suggest they stop often throughout the day, but the two old men were tough, just like Antonia had said. By nighttime, they had almost reached the outskirts of the region where Tasso wanted to send the men back to Elaiohori. But it was dark, and instead, they took to the brush and made camp.

As they sat to eat some of the cheese and bread Antonia had packed, Christo turned to Tasso and said, "That scar on your forehead. Where is it from?"

Tasso saw Niko give his friend an unpleasant look. "It's from the war, you goat! Don't bother him," Niko snapped.

"I know it's from the war. What happened?" Christo continued.

Tasso ran his finger across his upper brow. He had so many cuts and scars, but this one he would not soon forget. He didn't mind the inquiry, but before he could say anything, Niko offered, "You don't have to relive it. Forgive my friend for his ignorance." Niko put his hand on Tasso's leg as if to stop him from answering.

"It's fine," Tasso said. "I wasn't sure when I would tell you. The women were always around, and I didn't want to upset anyone." Christo sat up as Tasso spoke.

"The truth is ..." He paused, not knowing where to begin the story. Tasso closed his eyes to transport his thoughts. Lowering his tone, he confessed that when he enlisted in the army, his family was overcome with worry. He had placated his wife with the idea that his absence would be only for a short time. He shook his head in shame over his own naiveté.

"Things were worse than I'd imagined. I was a fighter in the front lines and placed in the heavy artillery section. Each gunner had two men assigned, a loader and a shooter. I was the loader." He paused. "I was in danger constantly."

Looking down, he continued. "One day, a cannonball landed close to me and exploded. My partner was killed instantly." In that moment, he recalled Margarita's face and felt a lump in his throat. "I was badly hurt but alive, and while I was being treated at the army hospital, the German army arrived to reinforce Italy's troops. The victory we'd celebrated against the Italians was soon overshadowed. Our army couldn't hold the line against the Nazis. We retreated and went back to our villages. Against doctor's orders I left the hospital and went with a group of soldiers to a port in Thessaloniki. We planned to board a ship there and travel to Egypt to fight the Germans in Africa."

"Africa!" Christo exclaimed.

Tasso nodded. "On our way to Thessaloniki, we came across a group of horses. We took them and traveled as fast as we could toward northern Greece. Once in Thessaloniki, we saw the last warship preparing to leave. It was full of soldiers. We got on board just before it left port. But as the ship headed out, Nazi planes came out of nowhere and dropped bombs. We were heavily hit, and the ship began to sink. I jumped into the sea and headed for shore." He shook his head as he recalled the carnage. "There were many dead. I swam toward land. Nazi planes continued to attack. Soldiers were killed in the water from flying shrapnel. It was terrible." He paused, remembering the voices of his comrades calling out in pain. "Men in a small boat pulled me out of the water, and not long after, the warship sank. Everyone aboard died." He exhaled deeply, feeling relief from sharing his secret.

For a while, no one spoke. Then Tasso added, "I was taken to another hospital and treated for this head wound. I stayed three days but left again and started toward home."

"How much you survived!" Niko said.

"Less than twenty made it off the ship," Tasso said sadly.

"My Lord!" exclaimed Christo.

"Had I been in my quarters—had I been any other place than on deck—I would have been killed," he surmised.

"I'm confused. Soon after we met you, you said you were trained as a secondary soldier, one who saw combat only at the border," Christo said.

Tasso looked down, ashamed. "Forgive me friends; I didn't want to worry anyone in Elaiohori. Many of my decisions haunt me." He thought of Margarita again but knew not to tell the men that her husband had been the gunner next to him. Then he said, "Mostly, I question why am *I* here and not them?"

"Because God needs you for something else," Niko said without hesitation. "We don't know our purpose until after the job is done."

Tasso looked up at the old man. "I just can't accept that I should be alive when those men are dead. The guilt is overwhelming." He had never expressed aloud the burden that screamed inside his head.

"Why guilt?" Christo asked.

"Those that died—they had wives and children too, talents to offer, gifts to offer this world. Perhaps they had homes to build just like me, plans for their futures," Tasso explained.

Niko reached over to touch his leg. "You carry an unnecessary burden," Niko advised. "Do your best to let it go. It's not easy, but your ability to reclaim a happy life with your family depends on your doing so."

He knew his friend was right, but it was hard to accept his words. Tasso looked at him and said, "I just hope Diamanto understands that I had to leave. She didn't want me to go. But how could I not help our country? Then what have I survived for? It seems no matter what I do, I'm needed elsewhere. I fear I won't be able to make an impact anywhere!" His voice rose in frustration.

"Go to your family. See your wife. Check on your house. Allow yourself to heal in the presence of your loved ones. The rest will come, Tasso," Niko said.

"Our sons, if they were on that ship … you said hundreds died." Christo's voice was shaky.

"Oh, Christo, I didn't mean to upset you. This is why I hesitated to tell everyone. I do not know whether they were on that ship. Remember, I was in a different infantry. I *volunteered* to go to Egypt," he said, trying to keep them optimistic.

"My son would have volunteered too," Christo said solemnly.

"Please, don't jump to conclusions. There is much movement in a time of war," Tasso consoled.

"He's right," said Niko. "You will drive yourself mad guessing. We best concentrate on the task at hand, keeping our sons in our prayers."

After a long silence, the men rested for the night. Although Tasso felt better after offering his whole story, he still felt terrible for lying to Margarita. He prayed for forgiveness and asked the Virgin Mary to comfort the young widow.

That night, perhaps because of a cleared conscience, Tasso dreamed again of Mandini and their wedding week. Celebrations had begun in Vassara on a Monday afternoon in a small home that belonged to one of Tasso's friends. The place was filled with guests who stayed up late into the evening with the Stamatopoulos clan that had come from Longastra for the nuptials. Tasso's cousin Dino, a skilled musician, teamed up with other cousins to play the lute, viola, and bouzouki. They showed off their skills, tapping feet and strumming fingers that moved across instruments faster than a bird. Each played a separate set of measures, impressing guests, who applauded the improvised solos.

While the air inside the home filled with delicious aromas of handmade pitas filled with fresh feta and kasseri cheeses, Dino and his band continued. Tasso even saw his mother crack a smile. Older men with clarinets sat outside the home's courtyard, slowly whistling traditional Greek love songs. He was the happiest he had ever been. Young men and women danced both inside and outside of the home as the two bands played. There were so many villagers in attendance that the celebration grew into the streets. Long trays of small, slim glasses filled with ouzo passed between guests. Late into the evening, he and his friends, along with Diamanto and her girlfriends, danced and sang, blissfully ignorant of time. As dawn approached, the party's roar calmed to quiet.

On Tuesday, Diamanto's parents, Kotso and Georgia, seemed to glow with delight at their home, which was located in the center of the village, just steps away from St. George Church. The small house built by Kotso's grandfather faced St. George's bell tower and had a large balcony. The lower level was made up of two large rooms, the kitchen and an eating area. Trays of food kept coming out of the lower level in a steady stream of activity. The same musicians from the day before played their clarinets and bouzoukis, offering favorite melodies for everyone to sing along to.

As if the celebration from the previous day had never ended, Tuesday's festivities maintained a steady flow. Diamanto smiled all day. Tasso relished her happiness, knowing the wedding erased her previously broken betrothal and completed Kotso and Georgia's duties to wed all of their daughters. The eldest daughter Pota was living in Montana, married to a man of substantial means, and their daughter Maria lived just up the street and was expecting another child. Diamanto's wedding was the last duty for the old couple. Tasso's future father-in-law came to him more than once that day to tell him how happy he was to have him as a son.

The week lost no momentum as Wednesday approached, and a party was given at the best man's house. Tasso's lifelong friend Yiani hosted the event, along with his wife Nikki, and the wine poured once more. Diamanto and her female entourage left early that night, leaving the men to their drunkenness while the ladies prepared for Thursday's customary tradition of baking wedding breads.

Tasso peeked in several times on Thursday to see his bride kneading and mixing. A white cloud of flour was suspended above her busy kitchen table. Hour after hour, they prepared loaves as part of the bride's dowry. Giggles of feminine laughter trailed from Diamanto's kitchen window. He smiled while watching them remove long wooden trays of sweet-smelling, golden-crusted loaves from Georgia's wood fired oven.

Friday was set aside for the delivery of the bride's dowry. Items were wrapped and tied with string and loaded onto donkeys that would carry them to the groom's family. Tasso knew his mother was eager to see what the Laskari family could offer in exchange for his hand. He doubted whether any of it could make her happy. Yet she was overwhelmed when beautiful tapestries, exquisite hand-embroidered tablecloths, bedspreads detailed with the finest silk threads, and select pieces of silver sent from America were presented to the Stamatopoulos family. Most valuable was a plot of land in nearby Magoula, provided by the bride's sister, Pota. Together with her husband, Diamanto's sister gifted the land to them. The property was the essence of Diamanto's dowry and offered little for Tasso's mother to mock. Tasso felt humbled at their generosity.

With the history of an unsuccessful betrothal, Tasso knew this particular day was especially delicate for his lovely bride. He did his best to treat her tenderly.

"Mandini, you know I don't care for one drachma from your father. Not a stitch of cloth from your mother, or a handful of land from your sister. You are mine forever, brought to me by God. There is no price on love." Her eyes beamed at him.

Saturday was quiet while both families prepared for the next day's event. His cousins planned a late-night "last drink to life" at the village tavern, but Tasso chose to stay only a respectful amount of time before excusing himself. He wanted to be fresh for the next day.

Finally, on Sunday, carrying wedding flowers for Diamanto, Tasso headed toward St. George. His family followed behind in a long procession. Keeping with tradition, he would receive his bride outside the church's main door. Walking up inclined cobblestones, he strode with purpose across the uneven road. Like their marriage that lay ahead, he thought, their journey would be an uphill struggle, filled with cracks and bumps to test their balance and shift their purpose. Still, he proceeded fearlessly, meeting each imperfection with the strongest of faith, believing that whatever came their way, they would prevail with trust in God.

As he got closer, Tasso glanced up at the bell tower adjacent to the church. Inside hung a newly fashioned bell made from copper pots donated by villagers. He smiled at the shiny, silent bell as if it were a friend, anxiously anticipating the joyous clamoring that would signal their completed vows.

Reaching St. George's courtyard, he saw the bride at last. Waiting with her family, Diamanto was wide-eyed and covered in white lace from head to foot. Her small frame was like that of a child, but through the veil he saw the face of the woman he loved. Tasso greeted her mother, Georgia, who kissed him on both cheeks, saying softly, "This is God's will." Her father embraced him before presenting his daughter.

Tasso looked down at Diamanto as they exchanged their first look as bride and bridegroom. His heart felt as if it would leap out of his chest for the little woman in white who had agreed to be his forever. She would be a good mother, he thought as she beamed back at him. Offering the bride her wedding bouquet, Tasso stood tall in his tan-colored suit. His jet-black hair was slicked back, and he hoped she found him handsome. Old ladies crossed themselves, and men shook hands, while little children stood in the courtyard watching the scene. With all eyes upon them, Tasso led his bride inside the church.

As they went through the main door, a chanter inside began traditional Greek matrimonial hymns, his deep baritone voice resonating through the crowd. A rotund priest with a long, white beard offered blessings while the shiny threads of his light blue embroidered vestments reflected the sun's brightness. Tasso's first cousin Antoni served as their religious sponsor, or *koumbaro.* The cousin placed two ceremonial white crowns of decorated leaves, called *stefana,* upon their heads. Symbolizing the status of king and queen of the couple's home, the *stefana* crowns were tied together with one continuous string of white satin ribbon, signifying their union as husband and wife. A few chuckles broke out among the parishioners when Tasso had to bend at the knees to keep the crowns in place on their heads. Perhaps a longer ribbon was needed, he thought as he smiled down at his flushing bride.

Holding long, yellow, lit candles, they joined hands with the priest, who held the Holy Bible in his right hand and led them around the altar table, circling three times. Singing the wedding hymn of the Greek Orthodox Church in a loud, pronounced tone, the priest proclaimed that he, Anastasios Stamatopoulos, and Diamanto Laskari were now wed with blessings of the church. A wide smile erupted across the bride's face as the bell rang loudly. When they headed to his relative's home for the reception, he looked to the sky and thanked God.

When the roosters crowed, Tasso woke with a happy heart and looked at the two old men sleeping. The dream of his wedding created a longing for simpler times, when there were no struggles between countrymen. The nostalgia provided energy for Tasso as well, filling him with a renewed sense of determination. He stood up to take a long stretch, anxious for the day to begin. They were closer to Vassara, he realized in the morning light, despite the pastel feathered haze that hung over the hills. The time had come to send the men home.

"You arise early as usual," Niko said, sitting up and looking into the morning sun.

"Thank you for helping me navigate this far. I think you and Christo should head back." He could tell the old man was relieved by this suggestion but was trying to hide it.

"Don't get ahead of yourself, Tasso. Are you sure?" asked Christo, now awake.

"I'm positive. We are well enough out of Elaiohori by now," he answered.

"Will it do any good for us to argue with you?" Niko asked.

"Not a bit," said Tasso, laughing.

"Well, let us share our rations this morning before you say goodbye." Christo started to set out some dried figs Antonia had packed.

As they shared a quick meal, Tasso decided to leave the men with a pleasant story. "Would you like to hear about my grandfather and King Constantine?"

"Of course!" replied Christo.

"Well," he continued, "as you know, my mother's family is from Longastra, high in the hills of Taygetos. Years ago, when my mother was a child, King Constantine visited the area for a hunting expedition. My grandfather Yiani was chosen to escort the king through the mountains because of his hunting experience. When the royal entourage arrived, they were dressed in fancy royal uniforms, all of them wearing dress boots of fine leather." He started to laugh as he recalled the story he had known since childhood. "Before long, the king's boots fell apart. There was no way the soft leather could stand up to climbing Taygetos's rugged hills and thick brush. So there they were, unable to continue. That's when my grandfather Yiani insisted on giving the king *his* boots so they could proceed."

"But what did your grandfather wear?" Christo asked.

"That's the part that makes me laugh! The king agreed, allowing my grandfather, a simple villager, to lace his boots onto the king's feet. In gratitude, King Constantine insisted his first officer, a man of high importance in the court, take off his boots and give them to my grandfather!"

Niko put down his handful of figs.

"So"—Tasso could barely get out the words through his

laughter—"while my grandfather continued hunting with the king, the first officer was forced to return to Sparta riding his horse with stocking feet!"

They shared a good laugh, but soon Niko's face turned serious. "So your family has been loyal to the king for generations?" There was some silence before Niko continued. "I understand. I used to be the same, as well as my father and his father. I'm not sure what happened to my Thanasi. I just hope it's not too late for him to make it out of this war alive."

Tasso hadn't realized his story would remind Niko of the problems with his son. He wished for a moment he hadn't said anything.

"War changes everything, Niko," Christo said. "Just pray Thanasi returns safe and alive, and the rest will come."

"Christo is correct," Tasso added. "War *does* change our lives dramatically—makes us appreciate simple things, like family."

Niko nodded and seemed to force a smile, which Tasso reciprocated.

"You are anxious to see your children, aren't you?" Christo asked him.

"More than ever." He paused. "And so, it's time. The only thing I dread is saying farewell to you fine men. Thank you for all you have done."

They stood up and exchanged embraces. Tasso helped them get their donkeys ready for the return to Elaiohori.

Before the two friends trotted off, Tasso walked over to Niko and said, "All will be well. I will pray for you every day."

"Thank you, Tasso," Niko replied.

"Be well, my friend, and enjoy those children!" Christo added.

He bade them farewell and watched the old men ride around the bend, feeling confident they would reach their village before nightfall. Turning to his own donkey, he took a deep breath.

Temperatures increased as the day continued, but the heat could not slow his pace or sway his happy demeanor. He traveled well past the noon hour, not stopping to take relief from the sweltering sun. When the afternoon began to show its first streaks of pink across the fading blue-colored sky, his heart beat faster. Traveling briskly around a large, green mountain, with two overlapping hills to his right, he saw what he yearned for—a little white speck in the dark, green carpeting of trees; it was the steeple of Agia Triatha, sitting at the crest of Vassara. Below the church lay a blanket of tiny houses, with clay shingled roofs and stone walls. Stretched over the landscape ahead, the village was once again real. The church called out to him in victory. Vassara was finally before him.

Chapter Five

On the outskirts of town, he didn't hear the faint clanging of sheep bells at first. But as the flock moved closer, their chimes grew louder. Tasso turned quickly and looked at the long line of sheep.

"Hello!" he called out. "Hello?"

There was no response. The sheep came closer, surrounding his donkey. He counted ten, fifteen, over thirty sheep, moving slowly about, heading across his path. He waited patiently, hoping their caretaker was nearby.

"Hellllloooooo?" he called out again, louder than before.

"Ahead, my flock, ahead!" a man's voice replied a few minutes later.

"Can you hear me?" Tasso got down from his donkey and pulled the animal's strap as he walked toward the shepherd that appeared.

The villager looked as if he had seen a ghost. "Tasso? Is that *you*?" the man asked, coming toward him with a limp.

Instantly, Tasso recognized his friend. "Petro!" he exclaimed, making his way through the animals to embrace him.

Petro had been injured at a young age, and his stricken leg still affected his ability to walk. Wobbling over to Tasso, his friend looked shocked. "Tasso! Where have you come from? Is anyone with you?" he asked.

"Just me," Tasso said.

"My God, we haven't heard from anyone in ages! No letters, nothing! We started to think all of you were dead." They stood together as Petro's flock swarmed around them. "Are you well? Your family will be so happy to see you!" he exclaimed.

Tasso made a wide grin, looking upward at the homes scattered across the mountainside. He felt his insides jump, knowing his wife and children were within reach.

Petro put his hand on his shoulder and asked, "Are more coming?"

Tasso answered, "I'm not sure." He shook his head. "But if I made it, there must be hope for others."

Petro looked him up and down. "How bad are you hurt?"

"It was far worse," he answered, looking down at his leg. "An infection persists in my leg, but I'll be fine," he explained.

"You must have traveled for ages to get here," the shepherd said, removing his tattered cap and wiping sweat from his forehead.

"I was on my way more than a month ago," Tasso explained, "but I ran out of rations and became dehydrated. Two men from Elaiohori found me. I stayed with them for several weeks until I was strong again." As Tasso looked up at the village he had feared he'd never see again, he focused his eyes on Agia Triatha. Thinking of his fellow soldiers and the time that had passed, he added, "There should have been more of us by now."

Petro put his arm around him, and Tasso looked into his friend's eyes sincerely. "If it weren't for the two men who found me, I wouldn't have made it."

Petro nodded, seeming to understand the marvel of his return. A wide smile erupted on his friend's face, and he said, "Well then, glory be to God! Let's get you to your family!" With a high-pitched whistle, he let out a call toward the mountain behind him. Within minutes two young boys came running.

Tasso smiled. "Vasili and Kosma? How they've grown!"

Petro rested a hand on each boy's shoulder. "Vasili, secure the flock! Kosma, run to the village square; tell them Tasso Stamatopoulos is back. He is alive! Then go to St. George's bell tower. Pull that rope until it breaks and let it ring loud!"

Tasso became overwhelmed with the reality of his return as his friend shouted, "This is a day of great joy!" Petro threw his arms up. "Go!" The boys took off running as Petro turned to Tasso. "I'm too slow with my bad leg. Go find your wife! See your beautiful children!"

Tasso wiped his eyes before mounting his donkey once more and then headed up the coming hill, toward the village school that led to the center of town. Lifting his head to the sky, Tasso made the sign of the cross and gave thanks to God. At last, he was home. In that exact instant, as if God was answering back, St. George's bell began ringing out in constant rhythm. Soon the villagers would arrive. With a repeated pattern clanging from Vassara's church bell to announce his arrival, Tasso trotted along the main road leading into town atop his donkey.

Over and over, he exclaimed quietly, "Praise be to God! Thank you, Virgin Mary." As he entered the town square like Jesus Christ on Palm Sunday, Vassareans spilled out into the cobblestone streets from their homes. They approached him with shock and surprise covering their faces. He scanned the crowd, looking for his wife.

Within moments, his donkey was absorbed in a crowd of old ladies wearing black, long-sleeved dresses, with black kerchiefs covering their heads, one a clone of the other. They reached for him, asking his name, but didn't wait for his answer. In that hopeful moment, he was everyone's missing son, husband, and brother.

A voice proclaimed loudly, "Tasso! This is Tasso!" He looked to his right and saw that one of the old women had fallen to her knees on the ground. She held her face in her hands as she rocked back and forth. He knew her. Tasso immediately descended from the donkey and ran to the old woman. He knelt down to embrace his mother-in-law, Georgia, who wept into his chest.

"Mother!" He held her as she cried.

Then a voice yelled out, "This is Tasso Stamatopoulos! Someone get Diamanto!"

Chapter Six

Run and get her!" shouted another person in the crowd. As children became part of the mob, he slowly got up and helped Georgia to her feet, looking anxiously into the faces of the children, hoping to find Elaine or George. Then he saw Kotso coming out of the village tavern with wide eyes and arms stretched open. The older man's walk quickly turned into a run across the square.

"Is it you, Tasso?" Kotso shouted.

Tasso was glad they hadn't seen him in his earlier state before he reached Elaiohori. "Father!" he cried, embracing his father-in-law.

"My God! A miracle of days! We feared most of you were gone."

"Only by God's blessings am I here. How is Diamanto? How are the children?" he asked.

"Oh, you blessed young man! Your beautiful wife and children await you!" he answered.

Then there was a shout from behind Kotso. "Uncle Tasso!" a young girl yelled, throwing her arms around his shoulders. Fofo was almost eleven now, the youngest daughter of Diamanto's sister, Maria. He gave her a tight hug.

"My mama said we may never see you again, but Auntie Diamanto promised you'd come back." The girl put her palms on Tasso's cheeks, which had become wet from tears.

"Sweetheart, look at you! Tell me, how is your auntie? How are your cousins?" Before the girl could answer, a youthful scream came from the road leading to the square.

"Baba! Baba!" His son and daughter raced toward him with joy and surprise on their faces. He ran to them.

George, now seven, was much taller than when Tasso had left. The boy's dusty kneecaps and forearms were covered with scrapes exposed by short pants and a faded short-sleeved shirt that was tattered on one side. His shoes were worn as well, and like all of the village children, George was thin. Despite malnourishment, the boy's thick black hair mimicked Tasso's and was parted on the side with a soft curl. His eyes, however, were his mother's—blue-green as the Mediterranean Sea. Tasso was overjoyed at the sight of his gorgeous son and could take his eyes off him only to notice the girl standing next to him.

Two years older, his eldest child Elaine had sprouted to more than a foot taller than her brother. With long, full curls, she also had the eyes of Diamanto, as well as her mother's fairer skin. She was growing into a true beauty. She was long-limbed and thin like her brother, and Tasso could tell both children weren't getting enough to eat. Elaine looked up at him with a sweet face. She cried as she reached for him. Still feeling twinges of pain from his injuries, he gathered all the strength he could to pick up both children in his arms, holding them at the same time.

"My treasure!" he pronounced, lifting his head to the clouds above. Louder and louder, he shouted the words, as if trying to send his gratitude directly to the heavens. "My treasure!"

Tasso turned and swung the children around, ignoring the pain in his back, the stress on his injured leg. He didn't care. Meanwhile, the large crowd around him grew even larger. Old women in black kerchiefs wept. But with the arrival of a woman running with a small toddler, the peak of his happiness was just unfolding.

A little woman wearing a wrinkled navy dress with a gray apron fought her way to get close to him. Her thick brown hair was feathered with what appeared to be remnants of flour; she looked as if she had been baking. He froze for a moment when he saw her, recognizing her lovely face and her sweet eyes, and was happier still when he saw the little girl in a faded pink dress whom she held in her arms.

"My Tasso!" Diamanto exclaimed, clutching their youngest with one arm and reaching for him with the other. He put down the older siblings and pulled his wife close. She folded herself under his left arm, and Tasso reached out to help her hold the toddler. He felt George and Elaine wrap their arms around his opposite side. He held his entire family together.

The little girl's large, raven eyes stared back at him with an innocent stare. She was his clone.

"Look who's here, Maria!" Diamanto said to the toddler, her voice trembling.

He looked into his daughter's eyes, identical to his own. Her soft, sweet face was surrounded by a head full of black curls. "Oh, my sweetheart!" he exclaimed as he kissed the little girl's soft cheek.

"She's perfect ... strong ... like her baba," Diamanto said.

"My Mandini! I'm so proud of you!" he said as he bent down to kiss the heads of George and Elaine. "What beautiful faces!"

Mr. Natakos came toward him carrying two chairs from inside his store. "Here," he said. "Sit with your family."

Tasso thanked him and set the chairs on the ground. With Tasso unable to take his eyes off his children and wife, they sat right in the middle of the square for a long while, as the crowd continued to grow. Mr. Natakos brought out more chairs, and soon there was a group gathered. Then people started to shout out questions.

"Where did you come from?"

"How far was your journey?"

"Did you see anyone else on the road?"

"Are others on their way?"

Tasso called out quick answers but grew uneasy as the people wanted more and more details. He was overwhelmed and looked over at his father-in-law.

Kotso looked back at him and stood up, saying, "Please, we are all so excited, but let the man breathe. He has had a long journey."

Relieved, Tasso looked down at George, who sat in his lap. Diamanto sat in the chair next to him, holding Maria, while Elaine stood next to him, her hand on his shoulder. He squeezed his daughter's hand as Kotso spoke.

Across the square, a man suddenly shouted a loud "Opa!" and two Vassareans with him began playing a lute and a violin. An impromptu celebration began. As villagers surrounded the musicians, a man outside the tavern held up a bottle of wine.

"Bring him wine! Bring him cheeses! Tasso, our hero!"

Within moments, a flurry of activity erupted throughout the square. Tasso noticed others standing off to the side, ignoring the events. Once the music began, he saw some of them leave. They were his friends' fathers, people he had known for many years. Why did they appear angry?

He looked again at Kosto, who came to his side and said, "Don't worry about that now."

St. George's bell continued to ring as local boys took turns at the rope. Eventually, along with the partying came questioning again. Tasso feared he'd be faced with another situation like the one he had experienced with Margarita in Elaiohori. The last thing he wanted to do was lie again.

Before he could decide what to do next, an old woman stepped forward and asked him about her son. Thankfully, he hadn't seen that particular soldier and truthfully told her he had no idea of his whereabouts. In return, the old woman asked what had happened to him. Tasso offered a brief version of his rescue, but before he could give any details, Kotso stood up and again addressed the group. His tone was kind as he spoke.

"I know you are all eager for information. We thank God for this blessed day that has brought our son home. May many more families in Vassara share the same joy!" The old man held his arm out to Tasso. "But my son-in-law, as you can see, is still recuperating and must go home to rest with his family. I'm sure you understand after what he has been through. Let's gather tomorrow and hear his news. For now, though, please let us head home."

There were a few murmurs in the crowd while Tasso watched the villagers' reactions. Many of them nodded their heads in agreement and got up from their chairs, offering well-wishes to him and Diamanto. Some, however, walked off abruptly and seemed upset.

The first crisp chill of the approaching night blew across the town square as Tasso bade farewell to a few more people, carrying George in his arms. Holding Elaine's hand, with George in one arm now, he walked slowly with Diamanto as she carried Maria. The little one had fallen asleep in her mother's arms. He smiled as they walked slowly with Kotso and Georgia beside them.

Tasso was anxious to talk to his wife alone, but for now, he was content to be with all of them as they made their way up the hill toward St. George. He couldn't wait to reach their home that sat outside the church's courtyard. In the stillness of the street, the evening wind whispered, and their shuffling footsteps created a rhythm. He and his Mandini exchanged a smile as they headed home.

When they reached the house, Tasso's in-laws asked the two older children to prepare the upstairs bedroom while they put Maria down. Kotso took the sleeping toddler into his arms from Diamanto, so at last, Tasso had a moment alone with his wife. He looked into her eyes to try to read her thoughts, but all he saw was affection, free from resentment. He was glad.

"You are well?" she asked.

He nodded silently while they embraced.

"Did you find him?" she asked.

"Nothing," he answered. She looked down, but he lifted her chin. "Diamanto, I had no choice but to go. This war is so much worse than we imagined. I may never know what happened to my brother."

"Then promise you will stay," she whispered sweetly.

He kissed her forehead and held her close.

Chapter Seven

Tasso didn't have the heart to put his children to sleep. He let George and Elaine spread across the foot of the bed while his in-laws sat beside them on wooden chairs. Late into the night, he told the family of his rescue. Mindful to leave out ugly details, he confessed the battle had been harder than he had ever imagined. Tasso explained what had happened on the boat to Egypt, the heroic actions of Niko and Christo, and the doting care he had received from Antonia in Elaiohori. Although his mother-in-law wept, Tasso noticed Diamanto didn't break down. He watched her solemn expression as she listened silently to his stories. As he concluded, he stroked the heads of his slumbering son and daughters.

"You were so blessed," Kotso offered. "Unfortunately, this place is no different. The divisions that existed before the fight are still a problem. But for now, get some rest." Taking Georgia's hand, his father-in-law stood up and kissed his daughter on her forehead. Tasso thanked his in-laws for caring for his wife and children during his absence, offering the first of many apologies for the difficulties they had encountered while he was gone.

After the older couple left the room, he looked over at Maria quietly sleeping and smiled.

"She is a peaceful child. Quieter than the others were," Diamanto offered.

"At last, a child that looks and behaves like me!" As they laughed, he noticed new lines on her face. Gone was the girlish grin, and in its place was an unfamiliar look of maturity, not bitter but serene and wise. He stared at her smile.

"What?" she asked, looking back at him inquisitively.

"There's a strength about you, a calmness." Tasso placed his hand on her soft cheek. "How?"

She looked down with a slight smile and touched the small gold cross around her neck. "My prayers," she said softly. "They are a large source of comfort."

"I wasn't sure ..."

"After you left, nothing seemed normal," she said, interrupting him. "My parents have been wonderful, but my true strength comes from praying to the Mother of God." Then she added, "I'm sure my resistance to you leaving weighed heavily on your mind, but I want you to know that in the end, I pulled myself together. I had no other choice." She paused before saying, "Tell me more about your search for Dimitri."

He exhaled, relieved, and said, "I'm proud of you, Diamanto. I'm sure things haven't been easy. As for my brother, there is no information as to whether he is dead or alive." He looked down. "But unlike you, I feel weaker than ever—confused, unable to find Dimitri, not understanding why I've made it this far. The last time I remember feeling sure about anything was when I was headed toward Thessaloniki. After the ship was bombed, something left me. My sense of conviction is gone." He turned away from her eyes. "I pray I don't appear as weak on the outside as I feel inside."

He felt Diamanto's hands on his as she said, "These are the hardest of days, Tasso, and they may become harder. I know once your leg heals, they'll call you back to fight." She became tearful. "All we can do is pray."

Tasso pulled her close and held her to his chest. He shut his eyes, kissing the top of her head.

"Go see Father Tomas tomorrow," she suggested. "Talk with him. See if he can ease your heart."

"You are my giant, Mandini. I love you."

"I love you too," she replied.

Tasso then got up and carried George and Elaine to heir beds, returning to Diamanto with a smile.

Just after sunrise, Tasso opened his eyes to the familiar surroundings of home. He gently kissed Diamanto's cheek and crept quietly out of bed.

The floorboards creaked underneath his feet as he walked into the next room to dress. When he headed downstairs to the kitchen, Kotso was at the table slicing bread. Georgia stood by the fireplace, making coffee.

"I'm surprised you're not still sleeping," his mother-in-law said, handing over a cup and saucer.

"Thank you," he said, inhaling the invigorating aroma. "Too much to do today. I want to see Petro and talk with some of the men in the square. But first I want to see Father Tomas. Do you think he's there yet?" He had pondered his wife's suggestion and knew talking to the village priest was the right thing to do. Hopefully, he thought, Father would have some answers.

Kotso looked up. "Oh, he's probably getting everything ready for tomorrow's liturgy."

"Thank you for the coffee," Tasso said, taking a last sip. "I didn't want to wake Diamanto. Can you please tell her I've gone to the church and will be back in just a little while?"

"Of course," Kotso replied. "Good to have you home, son." The old man smiled.

Tasso walked the few steps toward St. George anxiously, looking up at the bell tower, listening to the wind. Tall cypress trees that bordered the church's courtyard swayed from a deep mountain gust blowing across the area, filling his nose with fresh, fragrant air. He inhaled deeply while looking around. It was good to be back in Vassara.

The large church door was open, and the inside was dark except for the glow from a few lit yellow beeswax candles. Father Tomas's chants trailed through the entrance. Tasso stopped for a minute and made the sign of the cross as he adjusted his eyes to the darkened interior. He marveled at the church's ornate beauty as if seeing these renditions for the first time. For a simple village church, St. George's walls glittered in gold and silver, with large, elaborate icons of the Virgin Mary beholding Jesus Christ, the Last Supper, and the Baptism of Christ. Behind the altar, Father Tomas stood reading a Bible with his back to Tasso. A beam of morning light streamed through the window, shining across the inside of the church and onto the back of the priest's gold vestments, which draped to the floor, embroidered with satin thread.

"Father? Am I disturbing you?" he asked quietly.

Father Tomas turned around quickly and stretched out his arms. "Tasso! I was in Sparta yesterday and learned late at night of your arrival! Blessings to you, my son. Glory to God for your safe arrival!" He looked at Tasso's leg and asked, "Are you well?"

Tasso gathered he would have to offer an explanation for his limp a thousand times to concerned villagers. "I am well, thank you." He looked down at his leg. "This is the last of my injuries sustained at the border. It will take time to heal." As Tasso spoke, he noticed the old man's gray beard had grown significantly longer, resting over his broad chest, and had become striped with white strands, in contrast to the priest's balding head. Father Tomas's eyes were more wrinkled than he remembered. Time must have placed an abundance of burden on him as leader of Vassara's faithful. Surely his heart carried the concerns of every family. But Father Tomas was kind as ever, and his expression remained welcoming as his eyes sparkled blue and green.

"I am so glad you are home." He paused and stepped forward. "I gather you'll be leaving again once you're well?"

"Yes. I was hoping to get to Magoula before that," he confessed, wondering whether his intentions would come across as ridiculous to the wise old man.

The old priest let out a small laugh. "Doesn't sound like much recuperating if *that's* your plan. I know you better. You'll be up on a ladder even with those bandages."

Tasso smiled before asking, "Father, I wonder if you have a moment to talk?"

"Of course. Come. Let's sit." The priest directed Tasso to the front pew, which seemed the perfect place to unload his heavy heart.

Tasso made the sign of the cross as he looked at the beautiful, handcrafted solea in front of him and then into the eyes of the Virgin Mary holding baby Jesus that was painted above the altar table. He proceeded to tell the priest about the boat to Egypt, his rescue, his unsuccessful efforts to find his brother, and the guilt he carried for leaving his wife and children.

"I just can't grasp any meaning for things, Father. Why am I still here? Everywhere I go, I can't make a difference, as hard as I try. So why have I survived?" He felt sorrow building in his chest.

The priest put his hand on Tasso's shoulder and let the moment rest in silence for a while before answering. "Perhaps your frustration is part of your desire to control the uncontrollable. These feelings are not uncommon, especially for soldiers like you." He paused. "There are reasons the Lord has you here. These answers may or may not come to you in this lifetime. But know that you are a good brother, husband and father, friend, and son-in-law. Your time to succeed at God's plan will come."

While the priest spoke, Tasso looked down at his hands in his lap and turned them palm side up. He contemplated his fate as he stretched out his fingers, thinking about his longing to live a peaceful life as a builder and create beautiful things while raising his children. But the war had interrupted his plan. Would these hands be forced to kill a man before the fighting was over? Would he end up a prisoner, these hands bound together? Would he embrace his brother ever again?

Father Tomas interrupted his wandering thoughts. "Rest your leg … and your heart. Enjoy your family before you return to this monstrous fight." After a pause the priest added, "The answers will come."

Tasso nodded at the old man and thanked him for his time. As he passed through the dark doorway and reentered the morning light, he put his hands into his pockets, still feeling lost and unclear. He let out an audible sigh as he kicked a few rocks along his path. The priest meant well, he thought, but Tasso disliked the idea of waiting for answers.

Reentering the house, he was surprised to see the kitchen bustling with activity. Diamanto greeted him with a glorious smile and loving touch of the cheek, explaining that a steady stream of visitors had been stopping by with baked goods, fresh water from the river, fruits, vegetables, and homemade cheeses. The items were spread across the kitchen table, reminding Tasso of Antonia's bounty in Elaiohori.

"You met with Father?" she inquired, holding his arm. "I hope he helped."

He fashioned a smile for his wife and kissed her forehead, deciding to set aside his burdens for a while so that he could enjoy his family.

"Can you believe all of this?" Diamanto pointed to the baskets of eggs and the bushels of vegetables.

"Do they think I eat this much?" he joked to his wife. As they laughed, Georgia came over to him holding Maria. The toddler squirmed in her grandmother's arms, appearing agitated.

"Too much commotion for her, I'm afraid," said Georgia.

He bent down and kissed his daughter on the forehead.

"I'm going to take her upstairs for a nap. I can't believe Elaine is still sleeping!" Georgia said.

"Well, *I'm* awake!" said George, coming into the kitchen to latch onto his father. Tasso squeezed his son tightly. Georgia proceeded upstairs just as the door on the opposite side of the room swung open with a bang.

"Uncle Tasso!" A young boy burst in and ran to him.

"Nikola!" he answered, opening his arm to receive the light-haired boy and hold both of the boys together.

"I came from Verroia early this morning," he said with his big blue eyes beaming at Tasso. "I was helping Mr. Sgouritsa with his fields when we got word of your return. I told him we had to leave for Vassara right away!" The boy of almost twelve had matured in both body and mind, Tasso noticed, but despite Nikola's taller frame, Tasso still managed to pick up his son and nephew together.

"Oh, my dear boys!" He laughed and put them down as they shouted.

"What will we do first today, Uncle? Can I help? Can I come along?" Nikola asked.

"Me too!" said George.

"Have you had any breakfast, Nikola?" Diamanto asked as she put another slice of bread on George's plate.

"Well, I'm still a *little* hungry," Nikola replied. Tasso smiled as he watched his son and Nikola feast on the fresh fruit brought over by their neighbor, Mrs. Karangos.

Diamanto placed two fried eggs and bread in front of Tasso. He devoured his breakfast while the boys continued to pester him. Loving every moment of the commotion, he said, "Well, boys, I thought I'd visit my friend Petro this morning for a while. I need to talk with him." He winked at his wife, knowing both boys were friends with Petro's sons.

"Can we come?" Nikola asked excitedly.

"Let us come!" George insisted at the same time.

Tasso stood from the table and handed his empty plate to his wife. He kissed her gently and promised that he would return for lunch and that they wouldn't leave each other's side for the rest of the day. She nodded in agreement with a smile.

"I'll be gone only a short while. I have to ask Petro some questions," he added.

"I understand," she replied. "Here," she said, handing him a sack of bread, cheese, and pears, which he slung around his shoulder. "Take these to Petro and Katina. We must share some of this! I'll bring more to my sister Maria after the little one wakes up."

Tasso corralled the boys out of the house, heading out onto Vassara's streets. He walked in the middle of the two boys, listening to a constant chorus of well-wishes coming from balconies and doorways as villagers poked their heads out to see him. Although he felt uncomfortable with the attention, George and Nikola seemed to love it. He swung both boys on his arms as they walked on either side of him.

"Yiasou, Tasso! Good morning!" cried Mrs. Gianaras from her second-floor balcony. She waved down to Tasso and the boys with a large grin.

"Good to see you, Mrs. Gianaras! How is your grandbaby?" Tasso called up to the old lady.

"Well! Thank you!" she replied.

The boys practically skipped as they walked. When a door opened on the street level a few feet down the road, Mr. Gouris, the town baker, came out of a doorway holding a long loaf of bread. From the looks of his apron, Tasso guessed he had been up for hours, baking loaves for Christaki's general store.

"For you, fresh from the *fourno*!" Mr. Gouris said, handing the bread to Tasso.

"Thank you, Mr. Gouris! So nice of you!" He stopped and embraced the old man.

Mr. Gouris looked at the two boys and then back at Tasso. "Hold on a minute. Don't go anywhere. I'll be right back!"

The boys looked up at Tasso. They waited only seconds before Mr. Gouris returned with two smaller loaves, holding up one with each hand. "For you boys. Enjoy!" Nikola and George quickly took the breads from Mr. Gouris and thanked him politely. They turned to Tasso with wide-eyed grins, instantly devouring the bread.

"This is fantastic!" George replied with a mouthful.

"I love walking around with you, Uncle Tasso. You're famous!" cried Nikola.

The two boys continued to hold Tasso's hands while carrying what remained of their bread in their free hands. He chuckled as the boys returned everyone's well-wishes and repositioned the sack of food on his other shoulder while the boys swung on his arms, almost hanging from his limbs as they continued. He wasn't a bit bothered by the boys' active behavior. In fact, he relished their rambunctiousness, watching each of them try to jump higher than the other.

"I can reach my baba's shoulder!" George called out with pride.

"I can reach his neck—watch!" Nicola was able to reach higher.

Passing through the crowds that sat in the square, Tasso nodded to the men drinking their morning coffee outside the café and general store. He knew they were waiting for him.

"Thank you for your patience," he said. "I'll be by in just a little while to speak with you after I drop these packages off at Petro's."

They nodded in return. "We'll see you then," one of the men answered.

"Can I stay while you talk with the men about the war, Baba?" little George asked, looking up at Tasso as they moved out of the town square.

"I don't think so, George. I love having you boys with me, but I have to talk to these men alone." Sensitive to his son's feelings, Tasso rubbed his head and added, "We'll do something special later, I promise. Maybe we can read together." George smiled. "Your mother told me how well you behaved while I was away. I couldn't feel more proud. You're becoming a fine young man!" George's grin grew wider.

Nikola squeezed Tasso's hand and winked at him. Familiar with his nephew's mischievousness, Tasso realized Nikola thought he was mature enough to stay.

After a fifteen-minute walk, they reached Petro's house. His wife Katina came outside to greet them. She was a lovely woman, with a pretty face and a tall frame. Her dark hair was pulled back tightly from her forehead, and her genuine smile was contagious.

"Welcome, Tasso!" She embraced him. "Are you well?"

"I am. Thank you. It's great to see your beautiful family." Tasso smiled, handing her the tied bundles. "From Diamanto," he said. "We can't possibly go through all of this food before it spoils, even with George eating everything in sight!"

She smiled and took the parcels and motioned for them to follow her inside.

Tasso bowed his head to enter the short doorway.

"That was very generous. Please send my thanks to her," Katina said. "Come. I've made some halva." Katina's sons ran to see what was in the bags. She hustled them away and turned to Tasso, saying, "You should have seen the look on Petro's face when he came home yesterday. I've never seen him so excited! Sit for a while. The boys can play while you and Petro talk. I've already put hot water on for some chamomile tea."

"That would be wonderful," Tasso said as Petro entered the room with a smile and pulled out a chair for him at their table.

"Vasili, Kosma! Let's go outside," Nikola instructed. George and the younger boys followed him out the door to the field in front of the house. Katina reminded them to be safe, and within seconds the boys were chasing each other around an olive tree.

Tasso sat at his friends' table, looking around. It was a smaller home that sat just at the edge of Vassara, where the school was built off the main road. The kitchen had a tiny fireplace where Katina prepared the hot water. The scent of fresh chamomile filled the room and soothed Tasso's senses as much as Petro and Katina's friendliness warmed his heart. He could tell Petro anything and was never afraid of what the shepherd would think in return. A sense of calm came over him as he gazed out a small window that faced their side yard. A rush of hot air blew through. The sun was warming faster now, and cicadas hummed in the air, creating a rhythmic buzz.

They drank their tea while Katina unpacked the parcels. When they finished, Petro told him he needed to feed the animals. Tasso followed his friend outdoors, toward the animal pens.

"I know how badly you wanted to be there," Tasso said. "The fighting was worse than I imagined. You should know it was a nightmare."

Petro kept his head down as they spoke. He worked as he talked, shoveling feed into a large pail. "I gather you are an excellent soldier," he said. "It's no wonder you made it out alive. I would have been dead the first day."

"Oh, I don't know about that," Tasso answered, not wanting his friend to feel insecure. "Be glad you are here. Seeing men killed every day is a living hell." He shook his head as he recalled the carnage, grateful Petro didn't have to carry the same disturbing images.

"Trust me," Petro said, "I don't envy your situation, but watching Greeks grow suspicious of one another in the same town isn't easy."

"I saw some of that while I was in Elaiohori, this growing animosity for the king. How is this division here?"

"It's bad, Tasso. Some days it feels like the village is torn in two," he answered, picking up another load of feed with his shovel.

Tasso stood next to him and kicked the dirt beneath his foot, angry that the youth were so misled. "We've got to pull together," he insisted.

"One fight at a time, my friend." Petro rested his shovel and put his hand on Tasso's shoulder.

But Tasso couldn't be comforted. He shook his head. "Along with fighting foreigners, we struggle to save our country from ourselves? It's so wrong!"

"It was a matter of time, Tasso," Petro answered.

Tasso shot him a look.

"Don't misunderstand. I'm not excusing the behavior of these resistance groups, but when men are hungry, they'll do anything to feed themselves and their families."

Tasso retorted, "We are a mess, and we can't solve anything if we're not united."

"Has Kotso told you about how some of the farmers are hiding their grain? Instead of turning it over to the government for profit, they're stockpiling it, keeping a portion hidden so they can use it to trade. The bartering is unreal!" said Petro.

"I understand desperation," Tasso said, "but without organization, we can't defeat the enemy."

"Well, that's the point of these so-called resistance groups. I fear there's much more trouble ahead," Petro said.

"I agree." Tasso knew his friend felt the same frustration.

As Petro put down his shovel, he added, "Who will control this country when the war is over is anyone's guess."

That was what worried Tasso most, and Petro's words made it all more real. Recalling the coldness in some of the villagers' faces, Tasso knew the threat of something more horrible than the Germans was a real possibility.

"You should get out of here soon, Tasso. Go secure Magoula while you still can."

He didn't answer. His mind was still overcome by the idea of villagers hiding crops and turning suspicious of one another.

"Just be careful," Petro advised. "Watch your back."

"I will," he told him.

After spending another half hour with Petro, Tasso called to his son and Nikola that it was time to leave. They headed back to the center of town, where many were waiting for him.

George quickly ran off with his friends to play while Tasso pretended not to notice that Nikola had pulled up a chair to listen with the men outside Mr. Natakos's café. Kotso was there too and came over to sit next to him. Taking a long look at faces he hadn't seen in a while, Tasso made a mental note of the ones that were missing, wondering whether they were purposely keeping their distance.

By then, the noon hour was nearing, and bright rays of sunshine beamed through the trees that shaded the café's courtyard. Tasso told the group what he knew, understanding that up until his arrival, news had come to Vassara sparingly and with questionable authenticity. His information seemed a luxury to them. Just as he had explained to his in-laws, Tasso told them about the fight at the border and how he had made it back to the village. Inevitably, as in Elaiohori, a voice in the crowd called out to him about a missing son.

"Did you see Manoli? You were together on that carrier headed to Egypt, weren't you? That's what our son told us in the last letter we received."

Tasso looked back at the man who had nothing but hope in his eyes. "Mr. Natakos, yes. We were on the ship together, but we scattered like mice when the bombs hit." He paused before adding, "You all know how highly I regard each of your families. I want nothing more than to ease your worries, but I have little information on specific people. My brother Dimitri is still missing, so I sympathize for your heavy hearts. At the border, we were spread thin, and the retreat set us all apart. But I can't be the only one to make it this far. Give it time." He heard his words and stopped himself before continuing, asking himself how he could encourage patience among the villagers when he couldn't be patient himself, recalling Father Tomas's advice.

There was a long silence, and then a man said loudly, "Our troops should *never* have retreated!"

Tasso was ready to say something in return, but the old man was quickly reprimanded by others, including Kotso, who barked, "How can you comment on something you know nothing about? You were not there, my good man! It is unjust for you to pass judgment!" Kotso's voice was full of emotion as he rose from his chair.

Tasso reached for him to sit down and shook his head, requesting a passive reaction.

Murmurs broke out among them. Someone told Tasso to ignore the ignorant comments. Just as the outburst began, warm winds whipped across the high hills of Vassara, sending gusts of air through the town square. The air came through the trees like waves, sounding like the ocean shore crashing on the sand, as if nature was mimicking the unrest. Tasso raised his eyes to assess the clouds, wondering whether a storm was coming. Conversations continued a short while longer, after which Tasso suggested the men meet the following day to discuss things further. Midday was approaching, and the time for families to gather for the midday meal had arrived.

Standing up before departing, Tasso added, "There is much to do in order to prepare for the occupation. How much time we have left is anyone's guess, but it won't be long." He paused. "We can meet at the school tomorrow and discuss our defensive efforts."

Walking home, Kotso turned to him and said, "Don't lose faith in these people, or in the chance that you will find your brother."

Tasso put his arm around his father-in-law as the boys joined them, and they headed up from the town square toward home.

As soon as the group walked through the door, Kotso led Nikola and George to wash their hands. Tasso stopped a moment upon seeing Diamanto; she was noticeably different in appearance. She had on a newer dress and a clean apron. Her hair had been washed and brushed, and she smelled of sweet soap. But it was her smile that lit up his heart when he saw her.

"Mandini, you are simply glowing!"

She rested a basket of bread on the table when he took her into his arms and kissed her.

"I feel like I'm dreaming all of this," she said, "and I'm going to wake up and you're going to be gone again."

"I'm real," he said, kissing her on the forehead.

"Can I stay here in your arms forever?" she asked.

He smiled. For a while they were quiet, and no one disturbed them as they stood in their small, humble kitchen, embracing next to the kitchen table set with bounty. For that one moment, all was right in his world. He was home. The village was quiet. His wife's eyes were filled with happy tears that dampened his clean shirt just above his stomach. He closed his eyes as he held her and said another quiet prayer of thanksgiving, asking for strength in the uncertain time ahead.

Chapter Eight

The following morning, St. George's bell rang out loud, rhythmic chimes, announcing Sunday liturgy. Tasso sat up in bed and glanced across the room into the adjacent bedroom, smiling at his sleepy children, who covered their ears with pillows and blankets. The incessant clanging repeated every three minutes. Eventually, Elaine and George ran to their parents' bed, climbed over Diamanto's legs, and buried their heads underneath the covers.

"Time for church," he said happily, uncovering both children. "This is the Lord's day," he informed them.

"Uuuhhh!" moaned George, scooting under Diamanto's embrace.

"I'll be ready on time, Baba!" answered Elaine with a smile.

He studied her face, admiring his eldest daughter's increased beauty and feeling impressed as well with her maturity. "We will *all* be ready on time," replied Diamanto, stroking George's thick, black hair. "Elaine, check on Maria while I warm the water."

"Time to get up, George," Diamanto added. Her embrace turned into a shake. "Come," she said.

Tasso smiled at his wife's patience with the children. As they climbed out of bed, he thought about his conversation with the priest and hoped being in a spiritual setting would soften his frustration and uncertainty.

Less than an hour later, they proceeded up the street and entered the church. Tasso handed both George and Elaine a coin to place in a straw basket that sat on a marble slab in the outer narthex of the white stone building. He followed his children to venerate an icon of Jesus standing adjacent to a depiction of the church's patron, Saint George. Yellow beeswax candles stood erect in white sand on either side of the large framed icons. Making the sign of the cross, George and Elaine placed their candles in a standing silver bowl filled with the sand and kissed the icons. Diamanto lifted Maria to do the same.

All eyes seemed to be on Tasso as they moved about the nave. Feeling a little self-conscious, he nodded to Diamanto as he and George proceeded to the right side of the church with the men. Carrying Maria, Diamanto led Elaine onward, to the left side of the room with the other women.

Behind the altar stood Father Tomas, conducting the Divine Liturgy with what Tasso noticed to be a slightly weakened voice, or perhaps, he thought, the priest's voice only seemed less vibrant when compared to the strong vocals of the younger priest also present. Father Manolis, or Father Mano as he was known, had been ordained into the priesthood only months before Tasso's departure, after a large wedding celebrating his marriage to Evgenia, a lovely village girl who happened to be the daughter of Father Tomas. St. George had therefore become a sort of family business, with the nucleus centered in Vassara. Father Mano had thick, black hair and a beard to match. With his wide, kind eyes and gentle-looking, thin face, villagers loved him, even before he courted Evgenia. Tasso appreciated the young man's humility and believed he would make a good fit in their community.

As he watched the synergy between the priests on the altar, he was reminded of a group of handymen from Verroia, where he had once worked to fabricate the interior of a nearby church. He recalled how they had operated in concert as well, sometimes chanting hymns as they cut, carved, and hammered. Just like Tasso's fellow craftsmen, Father Tomas and Father Mano seemed to have a partnership of smooth perfection.

Father Tomas held the embroidered holy rectangle cloth and waved it above the altar table to begin the Creed. Tasso, repeating the words in unison with the rest of the congregation, looked up at the icon of Jesus Christ painted on the dome above his head. Saying the prayer like a thousand times before, he felt as if Jesus's eyes were peering into his soul, asking, "Where is your faith, Tasso?" Instantly, he was ashamed. Was his heart faltering? As if God was holding him accountable, Tasso hung his head in disgrace and realized that although other men had lost their lives in the war, he perhaps had lost something even more valuable: his belief.

Concluding the words to the prayer, Tasso became conscious that his insecurities had handicapped his mind. Indeed, Father Tomas was right, and only God knew the purpose for his survival. Faith needed to be foremost. In that moment, Tasso decided to focus on the task at hand, whatever it was and however often it changed without warning. He would inquire further about Dimitri, care for those around him, and carry out God's plan, whatever it came to be. He would love Diamanto and the children as much as possible before leaving again and would seek ways to bring the villagers together. He needed to convince them that unity was their only chance at victory. He knew it was a long list of aspirations, but he was determined.

Without warning, his mental manifesto was interrupted by a cold chill that covered his body. In his mind appeared the face of his nephew, Nikola. Extreme concern for the boy consumed his thoughts. Instinctively, he said a prayer for his nephew, not knowing why this thought wouldn't go away.

As the liturgy came to an end, Father Tomas stepped forward to deliver a short sermon.

"Let us rejoice at the wonder of God. Standing with us today is our dear brother Anastasios Stamatopoulos, home from the battlefront. He is here, alive! Let us all believe! Your sons, fathers, brothers, uncles, and friends need your prayers and faith. Let Tasso's return remind us of the power of our Lord." Tasso bowed his head, still thinking of Nikola, as the priest continued. "We face difficulty ahead, each man, woman, and child, but in that struggle, we strengthen our faith. We must remain united and put our differences with each other at rest. Turn your hearts to the Lord, dear friends. Only God will save us."

From behind him, Tasso heard whispering. He turned to see a commotion among a few men. One of them threw his hands up in the air and stormed out of the church. Four more men followed, carelessly swinging open the main door and allowing it to slam shut. Tasso turned back around, saddened. Even in the Lord's house, he thought, the unrest between villagers was relentless.

The older priest bowed his head and asked the congregation to come forward and receive *anditheron*. When it was Tasso's turn, he bent down and kissed the priest's hand while Father Tomas placed a piece of blessed holy bread into his palms.

When church was over, Tasso stepped outside into the sunshine, squinting his eyes at the instant brightness. The temperature had risen, and a palpable awkwardness hung in the air as the rest of the men exited the church after him. He hoped his good intentions and renewed spirit would pull him through.

When the women and children gathered outside, the mood slowly improved. He looked for Diamanto, who at last arrived, carrying Maria. He smiled at her, anxious to share the thoughts that had come to him during services. While reaching for his daughter, he leaned over and kissed his wife on the cheek. The little girl was asleep, and he brought her up to kiss the thick, black curls atop her head and then placed her over his shoulder. She was soft and warm, and he relished the feeling of her molding to his embrace.

He looked down at Diamanto and asked, "Remember when we were courting? I used to tell you that you were so tiny, I could fit you in my pocket. That's how I feel about Maria."

Diamanto laughed and wrapped her petite arm around his waist. They headed under the shade of a walnut tree in the church's courtyard. Relatives joined them, and they stood together talking. Elaine and Nikola chased George around the courtyard. Diamanto and her sister Maria spoke with their mother, Georgia, and Maria's daughter, Fofo. Tasso looked for Kotso and waved him over to where they stood.

Small circles of conversation complemented the ease of a Sunday morning schedule, when Vassareans allowed their animals to rest. Tasso overheard arrangements being made for families to share tables at each other's homes, combining what each family had to offer. The town baker, Mr. Gouris, provided loaves of fresh-baked bread for Mr. Melikakis, who in turn offered vegetables from his garden. Mr. Gouris's neighbor raised goats and therefore made cheeses, whereas another woman kept chickens. Together as a community, they ate from whatever means they had.

Kotso put his arm on Tasso's shoulder. "The whole village celebrates you, son. Father Tomas has asked me if you might have time to inspect the creek's bridge this afternoon. It needs a few repairs."

Tasso smiled at his father-in-law, who he could tell was full of pride. "Of course," he answered.

"I want to come with!" shouted Nikola as he stopped playing with the other children and looked at his uncle with desperation.

Remembering his vision during the liturgy, Tasso answered the boy with a smile. "That's quite a hike, but of course you can come. I will fetch you before I head out."

Nikola smiled and ran off.

After a meal that afternoon of bread, cheeses, and greens with olive oil and lemon, Tasso knocked on the green wooden door of his sister-in-law Maria. Nikola appeared within seconds.

"Ready!" the boy announced. "Where's George?" he added.

"With his sister. I thought we could go, just us two," Tasso answered, and a wide grin stretched across the boy's face.

They proceeded down the road that led to a small creek just outside the village's entrance. As they walked, Nikola asked, "Do you remember that letter I wrote to you while you were fighting the Italians?"

Tasso nodded. "You mean the one where you asked me to bring home an Italian prisoner so that he could do your chores and help harvest the olives?" he chuckled.

"Yes! You remember! Well," the boy said sincerely, "you should have brought one home … a prisoner, I mean. Then I wouldn't have had to work so hard in the fields. They could do all the hard work for us!"

Tasso put his hand on the boy's shoulder. "Nikola, I never would have taken a prisoner. You know that. Besides, didn't you get my letter in return? I wrote to you that I wasn't fighting any Italians. I was merely in the supply lines."

"Oh, Uncle Tasso, we both know better than that!" scoffed the boy.

Tasso paused for a moment in the middle of the street, stunned by the boy's accurate observation.

Deciding to change the subject, he said, "In the next few weeks, I'll need to check on the house in Magoula. Will you come with? I could use the help."

Nikola's eyes widened. "Oh, I'd love to! But don't you have to go back to fight?"

"I do, but my leg has to heal first. It still needs time."

"How long do you have?" his nephew asked.

"Not exactly sure," Tasso said, knowing the answer depended on so many things. "But I'm here for a while," he added to comfort his nephew.

"Oh, good!" said the boy, grinning.

Chapter Nine

It took Tasso and Nikola almost thirty minutes to reach the bridge beyond the furthest outskirts of the village. Tasso assessed the repairs and showed his nephew how he planned to strengthen the wooden beams that had weakened. He was pleased that the boy paid close attention and seemed interested. The work would take an entire day, perhaps two, he thought, and he promised Nikola they would paint the bridge together when it was done. The boy suggested a deep red color, and he thought that was a great idea.

"It will stand out in the green mountains, Uncle," Nikola said. "That way, when people are coming from Sparta, and they see the white of Agia Triatha's steeple, they will also see the red bridge and know how close they are to Vassara!"

"Already thinking like a builder!" Tasso said to the boy, rubbing his head as they packed up their things. A thick covering of white clouds moved fast across the fading blue sky. He smelled rain. "Let's get going," he said. "We might have a storm coming."

They walked the inclined road together, but before long, Nikola was lagging behind. Tasso called to him, and when Nikola didn't respond, he stopped and turned to find the boy pacing sluggishly and breathing heavily.

"Sorry, Uncle," he puffed. "I'm so winded today."

"That's all right!" Tasso said, slowing down to wait. When Nikola caught up, Tasso put his arm around the boy's shoulder. His own injuries had been bothering him for days, and the long hike to the bridge hadn't helped. He knew his wounds needed more pampering to heal properly, but his impatience prevented faster healing. Knowing he had a limited amount of time with his family, he felt there was just too much to do at home. Since Elaiohori, Tasso had resolved to pay the price of sustained pain, if he could get things done. He hoped the aching would eventually disappear, even though a part of him knew better.

"Maybe you should rest this afternoon," Tasso suggested, thinking he should do the same. Nikola nodded.

That evening, when Tasso and Diamanto went for a walk to the town square, the area was filled with the old and the young. A group of small children played tag around the large tree in front of Mr. Natakos's café while old couples sat on benches and watched. Kotso and Georgia were among them, smiling at Maria while she played with a friend. Groups of men Kotso's age were inside the café, gathered around small tables, probably talking politics, Tasso guessed. He could see the tremendous burden the old folks carried with their sons at war, worrying for their well-being while helping young mothers with the children. He felt sorry that their generation couldn't enjoy a calm period of time that would allow them to age happily. Instead, the war had brought hardship to what should have been years of tranquility.

George waved to his father while kicking a ball to a cluster of young boys across the square. Some older girls sat on the ground in a circle with a bundle of yarn, showing each other games with the string. Boys of the same age were playing nearby with a deck of cards, but Nikola was not there. He called to Elaine, who was showing little Yiani how to ride a rickety old bike. The front tire was nearly flat, but they persisted. He shook his head at their determination.

"That tire needs air. Let's see if we can fix it tomorrow," he suggested.

Elaine nodded with a smile. "Thank you, Baba."

"Where is Nikola?" he asked her, scanning the crowd of children.

"Aunt Maria says he's not feeling well. Something about a pain in his leg."

Diamanto squeezed Tasso's arm.

"George and I stopped by to pick him up on our way down," said Elaine, "but he was too tired, Aunt Maria said."

"Thank you," Tasso said to Elaine as she ran off to join the other girls. He turned to his wife. There was a look of concern on her face.

"My sister didn't say anything," she said. "This must have just come about."

"We'll stop by on the way home and check on them," he suggested, not wanting her to worry.

But when they arrived at Maria's later that night, Diamanto's sister confirmed the boy was ill.

"He developed a fever." She looked at Tasso with reddened eyes. Her voice was shaky. "And he keeps complaining about his leg."

He feared for the boy as talk of an illness affecting young children and their ability to walk had been widespread in recent months.

"Have you called for Mr. Antonopoulos?" he asked.

"Yes, he was here," Maria answered. "The soreness in his limbs is quite concerning, he said. We are not to wait more than a few days before taking him to Sparta's hospital." She started to cry. "Oh, my poor Nikola!"

Diamanto hugged her sister. Tasso was disturbed by Mr. Antonopoulos's assessment and stepped inside to see his nephew, but the boy was asleep. He covered his chest with the thick woolen blanket that rested across his waist and made the sign of the cross over the boy's body before exiting the room.

"You come to me if anything worsens, Maria, no matter the hour," he told her as they walked through the large door.

She nodded to him with streams of tears running down her plump cheeks. Ever since he'd met her, Maria had always seemed to be in a blaze of worry, even when her children were healthy. An unadorned village woman with a rotund frame, Maria was adamant about cleanliness but cared little for frills. Strands of gray prematurely streamed through her black hair, making her appear much older than the two years that separated her and Diamanto. For Maria, a clean, well-run household was paramount. As if she had willingly let go of her youth, Maria cared little for her own appearance and was more concerned that her kitchen was scrubbed daily.

Diamanto was less stringent and cared more about having a bouquet of wildflowers on her table. Ever since marrying her, Tasso had been both amazed and amused at his resourceful wife, who could reuse a discarded garment or gather elements from nature to make their home look pleasing. With his wife's shapely, petite body and love for all things beautiful, Maria and Diamanto were widely opposite in appearance and personality. However, despite their visible differences, the two were tighter than ever, and he knew his wife would absorb Maria's worry. In all his life, he had never witnessed a greater love between siblings.

Maria especially loved Nikola, which Tasso was sure would add to her distress. While her husband was off fighting, Maria relied on Nikola and his older brother Kosta more than the others. Of all her children, including young Fofo and little Yianni, Nikola stood out as the most gregarious. In addition, the boy had an undeniable artistic talent. From the time he was young, he and Tasso had often sketched together. While making plans for the house in Magoula, Tasso had involved Nikola with design ideas, and he hoped one day to make his nephew an apprentice along with George.

The next twenty-four hours faded into a blur as Nikola's condition worsened. The family rallied together. Kotso and Georgia helped Maria care for Nikola while the other children, Kosta, Fofo, and Yiani, were taken out of the home for fear they might contract Nikola's undiagnosed ailment. They would stay with Tasso and Diamanto. With a rambunctious group running through their home, Tasso helped his wife put blankets on the floors, creating sleeping space wherever possible. Little Maria seemed to love the chaos and giggled as she ran through the rooms, chasing her cousins. Diamanto worked diligently while they waited around the clock for the boy's fever to break.

Other villagers helped as well. Maria's laundry was washed by a neighbor. Another friend brought fresh water from the well. Father Mano came to anoint Nikola with holy oil and said prayers of healing over the boy. A short, quiet nun named Ourania brought Maria a small icon of the Virgin Mary to keep at Nikola's bedside. Tasso was endeared to Ourania and remembered her husband well. She had been widowed at a young age and found her strength in religion. Ourania's eyes glistened as she told them all would be right with the boy. But Tasso, cautious of his nephew's worsening condition, knew he needed to get the boy to the hospital. He had already concluded that he would escort Nikola and Maria to Sparta.

The next day, Tasso asked Petro if he could borrow his carriage for the trip. Diamanto planned to remain in the village to care for the other children while he and his sister-in-law were in Sparta. He resigned to the fact that they would be gone for an undetermined amount of time.

Later that afternoon, their satchels were loaded into the carriage, and early the following morning, Tasso carried his sickly nephew and placed him carefully in the cart, wrapping blankets around him from the waist down. The boy was limp and pale, too weak to talk. Tasso's heart broke as he saw Nikola's pathetic state; he was astounded by the quick onset of illness. *Just the other day, we were laughing,* he thought, trying to make his nephew comfortable. Villagers gathered outside the home to wish them a safe journey. Tasso climbed in the front of the carriage after helping Maria settle herself and gripped the reins. The villagers waved farewell, sending Nikola blessings for a healthy return. Maria was an emotional mess as she waved back at her parents and sister, holding onto her sickly son.

"Be well, Nikola!" George shouted to his cousin, running alongside the carriage, trying to keep up. "We love you. Come home soon!"

Tasso's last glance back showed his mother-in-law Georgia making the sign of the cross with Kotso's arm around her. "God bless you," they cried.

After several hours' journey, Tasso made his way into town with Maria and Nikola. The closer they got to Sparta, the more consumed with worry he became. The one and only hospital in Sparta was a chaotic place, with no sense of order. Greeks of all ages came into the white stone building with illnesses and injuries of all kinds, wailing, holding bandages on bloody wounds. Obtaining attention from medical staff was difficult. When Tasso walked through the main doors carrying Nikola, they were told to sit and wait. Finally, after over an hour in the noise and confusion surrounding them, a nurse came to him.

"Over here," the woman in white said.

Tasso stood and carried Nikola, with Maria following closely behind. The short woman in uniform motioned for him to place his nephew on a table just off the waiting room. She directed the staff, who began tending to the boy while she asked a myriad of questions. While Maria continued to cry, he explained the details of Nikola's symptoms. The woman took notes on a clipboard and left, telling them that a doctor would come momentarily.

After another half hour, a short man with gray hair wearing a doctor's coat approached them. The man's small round glasses emphasized his serious expression, and he spoke in low monotones, appearing exhausted. The doctor rubbed his forehead repeatedly, as if he was trying to relieve a headache. He looked into Nikola's eyes and mouth and felt his pulse while Maria wept over her son's body. Tasso spoke to the doctor directly but politely, ensuring that the doctor understood he took personal responsibility for his nephew's care.

"We will run some tests" was all that the doctor said.

Tasso took Maria to a rented room across the street. Settling his sister-in-law into one of the two bedrooms available, he returned to the hospital to see if there was any progress. Maria seemed devastated, and he knew she needed to rest, or she too would require medical care.

Many days later, as they sat waiting in a hallway on two wooden chairs set outside a room where Nikola rested, the same doctor came out to speak with them.

"I'm afraid the boy's troubles are coming from the onset of polio," the physician said without feeling.

Maria let out a loud wail and collapsed into the arms of a nurse, sobbing. Tasso did his best to keep his composure while anger, denial, helplessness, and doom fought against his attempts to remain strong.

"There are some therapies," the doctor added, "but more importantly, there is an operation that may save the boy more assuredly."

Tasso pulled the doctor to the side, whispering that he should not offer further details. Instead he requested they talk in private. Tasso turned to his sister-in-law. "I'll be right back. Let me discuss this with the doctor. It's good that we're here and we caught this early, right, doctor?" He put his hand on the white coat sleeve of the physician.

"Yes, but …"

Tasso stopped him. "Well then, see, Maria? We have time on our side. Let me ask some questions, and I'll return to explain our next step."

When they stepped into an empty room next door, the doctor's tone became tense. "The best way to save the boy is to remove his leg. I've scheduled the surgery for tomorrow," he said.

Feeling blood rush to his head in a pulsating throb, Tasso shouted, "That procedure will be canceled at once!" Two nurses came through the door of the room, hushing him.

"Amputation is the only sure way to save this boy's life!" the doctor continued.

Tasso lowered his volume, but his fury remained. "You will *treat* him with whatever medicines you have. Do you hear me?" Taking a deep breath, he tried to calm himself.

"Even if we don't amputate, we still have to open up the leg to see how severe the infection has become," the doctor advised.

"You will not make any conclusions regarding amputation without my authority." Tasso took another breath. "And furthermore, I will be present at any and all procedures regarding my nephew."

The pensive doctor seemed to forget his own manners and raised his voice as well. "I cannot allow you to be there! That is against all hospital protocol."

After a long, heated exchange, the doctor relented. Tasso was victorious.

"Then it is settled," Tasso stated. "Tomorrow's procedure will be investigative *only*. Your protocols will have to be put aside."

As his nephew was prepared for sedation, Tasso settled Maria into the waiting room. He bent down and gave her a kiss on the cheek and then returned to Nikola's room, where the doctor was obviously frustrated with his presence.

"You understand we have no idea what we will find," he said to Tasso.

"I understand," Tasso answered.

"Here. Wear these garments." The doctor motioned to a nurse, who handed Tasso a small, folded bundle. He took the mask and surgical garments.

Nikola's eyes were beginning to shut, but Tasso leaned over the boy and whispered, "When this is over, I am going to buy you a new bike!"

A smile began to form across Nikola's mouth just before his eyes shut. Tasso leaned over and kissed him on the forehead before they wheeled the boy away.

The sterile room was quiet as the surgeon spoke softly to the nurses, who handed the doctor requested instruments. Tasso was careful to remain out of the way while staying vigilant at his nephew's side, quietly reciting in his head the words of a hymn dedicated to the Mother of God, asking Her to intercede with healing and strength. As he prayed, his mind traveled back to when Nikola was a young boy, accompanying him on a job at a church in Verroia. Joining his uncle every day with other craftsmen to design, plan, and build the holy structure, Nikola had never left his side.

"Why do you sing hymns, Uncle?" asked the young boy who loved to pick up his hammer and pound nearby rocks, imitating the workers' gestures.

"Their words give me peace while I labor," he told him.

"I bet God can hear you!" Nikola answered.

Tasso hoped Heaven could hear him now, as he prayed directly to the Mother of Jesus. *Please, holy Mother of God, bestow upon this boy your healing powers. Let him walk again; let him keep his leg; let him live a long, healthy life of love and happiness.*

Tasso remained frozen for a while. Tears streamed down his face and he let his anxiety pour out. Closing his eyes, he remembered the feeling he'd had in church while looking at the icon of Jesus. He recalled how Nikola's face had come into view and how he'd suddenly felt that the boy needed protection. As it all began to make sense, a cold chill ran through his body.

The surgeon looked up and nodded with a slight smile. This was the first pleasant expression the doctor had made, and Tasso knew it was a good sign. The physician announced, "We will close him up now."

Tasso emerged from the operating room white as a ghost, but smiling from ear to ear.

Maria jumped up from her chair, asking, "What happened?"

"No amputation. It will take time, but they will treat him with therapies," he told her happily.

She rushed into his embrace, weeping.

Several hours later, when Nikola regained consciousness, Tasso and Maria were waiting at his bedside. The boy let out a moan.

Maria sprung from her chair. "My sweet boy. We're here."

Tasso took his hand.

"What happened?" Nikola asked groggily as he lifted his head slightly and tried to look down at his body.

Tasso smiled down at his nephew. "You will be riding that bike," he told him. "Your leg will heal, Nikola."

The boy closed his eyes and smiled, resting his head back on his pillow. "Thank you, Uncle. Thank you," he said, falling back asleep. Tasso put his head onto the boy's chest and wept, thanking the Mother of God for this blessing.

While Nikola spent weeks recovering from surgery, Tasso resorted to having his own leg examined. He was having an increasingly harder time ignoring the pain and suspected the infection had gotten worse.

"Why didn't you let me examine it earlier?" the doctor asked.

Before Tasso could answer, the doctor added, "I know—your nephew. But Nikola is coming along well. He still has a long way to go, but we were lucky to have caught the disease in time." He put down his clipboard. "Let's take a look," he said.

Tasso sat on the examining table and pulled up his pant leg to reveal the wound. The doctor slowly removed the bandages.

"Quite infected," he said. "I want to see you every other day while we treat your nephew."

Then Tasso asked the question that was burning in his mind. "How long before I can get back to my unit?"

The doctor didn't take his eyes off the leg but shook his head in reply. "Not for a long while," he answered. "Your leg needs to make substantial improvement. I assume you've kept it as clean as you could, but medication is needed." He looked at Tasso. "Infections come back easily. I don't want this to get worse. We'll have the necessary document signed for your superiors."

Tasso did not challenge the doctor's assessment. He was glad he'd have more time for his nephew and family but knew he needed to get back to the fight as soon as possible as well.

When he met up with Maria again, she looked at the papers he carried and asked, "What's that?"

Tasso flipped through the three pages that ended with the doctor's signature. "It's a report of my health, addressed to the army offices," he told her.

She looked up with a surprised expression.

"It says that I can't resume duty for a period to be determined by the hospital." He shook his head at the papers, grateful for the doctor's efficiency but wondering whether the man was merely trying to keep him out of the fight.

"Glory be to God," she answered.

When Tasso returned to his rented room across the street from the hospital that evening, he sat quietly and composed a letter to Diamanto. He happily wrote what was finally a note with real developments. He feared earlier messages had left her uncertain. At last he bore good news.

My dearest Mandini,

I pray this message reaches you quickly. Although our predictions of Nikola's illness were proved correct in a confirmation of polio, it has been determined also that our nephew will be treated with medicines and therapies. He rests comfortably with your sister at his side as his fever regresses. His healing, we are told, will take time, and we are still in Sparta an indefinite amount of days, but as he progresses, all is well. Your sister is doing much better than when we first arrived.

As for me, I have taken the opportunity to have my own wounds assessed and was informed that the infection in my leg is still present. But don't worry. The same doctor who treats Nikola also takes care of me with great attention. You will be happy to know that he has documented my condition for departments of the army. I shall present the doctor's paperwork tomorrow and, at the same time, inquire about my brother.

As you know, it is important for me to let them know I am still alive and will return to my unit as soon as I am able.

Meanwhile, I am optimistic that I may learn more of Dimitri's whereabouts.

Please spread the news of Nikola's blessing to our family and friends in Vassara. As always, give Elaine, George, and Maria as well as your parents my deepest love and affections. I pray you are well, dear wife, for I miss you so.

I will write again soon.
All my love,
Tasso

He closed the letter and put it into his breast pocket to pass along to a man who would be traveling toward Vassara that week.

The morning sun shone strongly the next day as Tasso walked to the municipal building not far from the hospital, carrying his medical papers. He was not nervous but was anxious to set the record straight with the authorities and inquire about his brother. As he limped up the marble stairs and entered the building, he saw an elderly uniformed man sitting at a small desk.

"Yes?" the man said, glancing up from an array of paper scattered about the desk.

Tasso introduced himself and explained his purpose, showing that he had written documentation of his injuries. The man looked him up and down and then pointed to a hallway and instructed him to wait outside the first office door. Tasso made his way down the narrow hallway, passing an armed man who stared at his limp. When he reached the office, a man on the inside got up from his desk and opened the door, telling him to come in and sit down.

"Good morning. Your name?" he said.

Tasso sat down and proceeded to answer an unending line of questions. He took his time, recalling each detail, from his first injury at the border onward. The officer took notes as Tasso spoke, and when asked for any and all new information, Tasso even included his intentions to move to Magoula while waiting for orders and his medical release. Unsure of how long they would be in Sparta or Vassara, he didn't want to appear as though he were hiding anything.

The officer reviewed his medical papers and agreed that the doctor's guidelines would be followed. Tasso was told to report back each week, and he signed a paper agreeing to do so. Surely Tasso would be of no use to the army if his infection became worse.

At long last, he inquired about his brother.

"His name?" the man asked.

"Dimitrios Stamatopoulos," Tasso replied.

But instead of offering him any information, the officer directed him to yet another man inside another office. Tasso thanked him and proceeded down the same hallway to the third door. The door to this office was open, and the man sitting inside was much older. He appeared weary. The officer asked Tasso to repeat his brother's name and then slowly pulled out a large ledger many inches thick, with a black cover from a desk drawer. Slowly turning the parchment sheets of the book, the officer rubbed his head.

"When was the last time you heard from him? Where was he fighting?"

Again hit with a long line of questions, Tasso answered as precisely as possible, hoping to obtain an answer. After several minutes of running his finger up and down the lists of names, the officer stopped at an entry and slowly followed the dotted line across the page to the right-hand column.

"Dimitrios Stamatopoulos of Longastra?" he said.

"Yes!" Tasso replied eagerly, sitting up in his chair.

"Your brother is listed as missing. Last placement in Albania well over a year ago." The man paused but then continued. "There is a notation in the ledger indicating that his company may have been taken prisoner. However, he is not formally listed as a prisoner." He paused again. "I'm sorry, soldier. That's all the information I have."

Tasso was immobile for a moment. He felt blood drain from his head, and at the same time, a sharp pain struck his temple. For a second, he thought he might pass out. Tears flooded his eyes, but he fought them back and took a deep breath. What he had suspected all along was true. Dimitri was gone. No one knew whether he was alive or dead or whether he had been taken. For the first time, Tasso was glad his parents weren't alive to feel the pain of a missing son. This would have broken their hearts. But he had to get word to his sister and his other brother. He stood up and shook the man's hand, thanking him for his time.

Walking out of the municipal building in a semi-stupor, he was struck by the bright sunshine that spread across the building's courtyard. Pausing at the top of the large marble steps, he squinted at the sky, feeling sadness, anger, and frustration. Where was Dimitri? Could he be a prisoner of war? Had he been killed? He shook the horrific thoughts out of his mind and descended the steps slowly. His leg pain persisted. His head throbbed. His broken heart ached. Walking down the stairs with difficulty, he proceeded to exit the army property through the front courtyard. Trying to contain his grief, Tasso reminded himself of Nikola's miraculous recovery. He was thankful his nephew had been able to keep his leg. But although one tragedy had been averted, there remained many uncertainties.

Chapter Ten

Over the next several months, Nikola underwent rehabilitation. Tasso noticed his demeanor was remarkably upbeat, despite an array of therapies that included vigorous exercises, traction devices, and both hot and cold compresses used to restore his leg muscles. Nikola's doctor appeared adequately optimistic but continued to warn Tasso that at any time his nephew might take a turn for the worse.

He and Maria scheduled themselves in alternate shifts so that Nikola was rarely alone. Whereas Tasso went to the hospital early each morning, Maria came after lunch and stayed until evening. Every few days, Tasso saw the doctor and had his own injuries examined. His bandages were changed, and various ointments were applied.

One afternoon, while Maria was at the hospital, Tasso took a long walk from Sparta's center, up the main road that led past St. Demetrios Church to the outskirts of Magoula. Tasso struggled with his limp up inclined streets to take the trip he had longed for. Magoula was a small village, about a twenty-minute walk from Sparta's center, made up of farms and orchards. He had wanted to get a glimpse of his partially completed home ever since returning from Albania, but other priorities had taken precedence.

The property of roughly ten acres began just off the main road leading from town. His neighbor's property across the road was thick with green trees, and Tasso looked at the flourishing orchard with envy, admiring its growth. His land on the other side remained dormant, awaiting attention.

As Tasso approached his home, a young boy he recognized came down the dirt path to meet him. Panouli Sanos was fourteen years old and lived in a small house next to Tasso's land, where his family maintained a small farm.

"Mr. Tasso? Is that you?" the boy asked.

"Panouli! You've grown taller!" Tasso exclaimed.

"Soon I'll be old enough for the fight!" the dark-complexioned boy replied. "What are you doing here? Are you back from the war?" The boy looked at Tasso's leg as he came closer. "What happened?" Panouli asked. "Were you hurt?"

Tasso briefly explained about Albania, his leg, Nikola, and the treatments his nephew was receiving in Sparta, as well as his plans to fix the house before his new orders arrived.

"Unbelievable!" Panouli said. "My parents will be happy you're back!"

Tasso walked with Panouli around the perimeter of the property with excitement. He had feared so often that he would never see his home again, but at last, he saw it.

So many emotions exploded at once. He felt grateful, happy, eager, and impatient all at the same time. How he wished there was nothing more on his agenda than to leisurely and meticulously finish every inch of his partially constructed home. He took a long, deep breath and sighed.

Panouli asked, "Good to be back here, Mr. Tasso?"

"This place is my release," he answered, looking side to side, feeling as if his worries didn't exist while he was here. But as the reality of his life returned to his mind, he started to take mental notes of the home's needs. With a large balcony built to run the full length of the level upstairs, an almost perfect view of Mount Taygetos was the prize of the home. He was pleased with his work and felt proud that his design and construction had come together successfully. It was a beautiful house, and he couldn't wait to live in it.

Walking through the courtyard, he stepped into a large, almost completed kitchen with a connected room for eating and sleeping and a small second room for storage. As he remembered, the windows needed to be finished, but the walls were solid.

"It's amazing," Panouli said.

Tasso couldn't help but agree as if someone else had done the work. When they walked back through the courtyard toward the gate that led out to the dirt road, Tasso asked Panouli to gather some of his preteen friends who could help with weeding and removing debris from the fields.

"I can't pay them much, but rest assured, I'll figure out something," Tasso told him. "They will be busy!" After looking around one last time, he said, "I wish I could stay here all day, Panouli, but I have to get back to my sister-in-law and Nikola."

"Good to see you, Mr. Tasso. We'll be ready to work when you get here!"

"Thank you, Panouli," he said.

By now it was midafternoon, and Tasso headed for Sparta's center. It took him a while to reach town, limping slowly. His leg pain grew worse. Heading for the busy area covered with small cafés, he looked around at the town square, imagining the evenings he and Diamanto would spend there with the children once the war was over.

A municipal building stood at one end, with the Greek flag flying over its yellow roof. There was an open area on the opposite side where small children chased each other. Tasso stopped at a newsstand next to a line of cafés and picked up a paper to take to the hospital. The front-page headline was a distressing confirmation of stories spreading through town regarding an increased food shortage in Athens. Reading of an Allied blockade that had cut off food lines to Nazi troops, he was saddened to learn the efforts had backfired against the already suffering Greeks. As he continued walking, he scanned the article; it detailed extensive pilfering of villages outside Athens and described the thievery of the Axis powers, who stole livestock, grains, and produce from small towns near the country's capital. Villages on the outskirts of Athens were most affected, the newspaper said, and those who resisted were killed. He clenched his jaw in anger, infuriated by the escalating tragedies.

An old man passed him on the promenade, carrying the same paper. His expression was urgent. "Our people are starving! There is no food!" the old man cried, shaking the paper in the air as he passed Tasso.

Limping across the square in throbbing pain, Tasso knew he had to rest. After sitting down at a table in an adjacent café, Tasso spread the paper out in front of him. The unfolded headline stated, "Famine in Athens," with horrific photographs of children lying in the streets of Syntagma Square, outside Parliament. His heart sank. One caption stated that thousands were dead and dying, leaving the rest to scavenge for food while conditions worsened. Overwhelmed by the images, he put his elbows on the table and rested his face in his hands. Tears came without warning as he found himself unable to hold back his grief. In addition to his heartache for Nikola, this seemed unbearable. His hands began to tremble, and he found himself drawing inward, to the darkest place in his mind, where sadness, fear, and anger lived. How could this happen? The poor children! Unlike what he had seen at the battlefront, the unjustified suffering of little ones ripped at the steady but vulnerable psyche he previously had been able to sustain, even with Nikola's fate in the balance. He missed his wife, Elaine, George, and Maria. He feared for his brother Dimitri. He dreaded leaving his family again. It was enough to break him.

But something inside his heart would not allow his spirit to give up. Like the glow of a small candle in a vast, dark cave, there flickered a light that somehow was enough. He knew falling into despair would cause everything else to crumble. Lifting his face to the sky, palms together in prayer, he whispered, "Please, Mother of God, show us the way through this." Eyes closed, he sat silently weeping and praying until a young boy wearing a white apron appeared next to his table.

"Sir? Can I get you something? Would you like a coffee?" The boy spoke hesitantly as he placed a tall glass of water on the table next to Tasso's newspaper.

Tasso looked up and forced a smile. "No, my dear boy." Reaching into his pocket and pulling out a drachma coin, he added, "I just needed to sit for a while. Thank you for the water." He placed the coin in the child's hand and patted him on the arm.

"Thank you, sir!" the boy said with surprised expression.

Tasso stood up and straightened his jacket. Not wanting Maria and Nikola to see his reddened eyes, he tried to gain composure while repeating the prayer in his head, hoping God would hear his plea.

As he came up on the corner where he was to turn for the hospital, he saw a large crowd gathered outside a municipal building. Men and women stood waving white slips of papers in their hands, looking impatient and yelling out.

"Give us one—no, two! We have plenty of room!" a woman said.

"I have no children! Send me one!" another pleaded.

There was a woman in a stiff white Red Cross uniform trying to put the aggressive people in line. "Patience please! Everyone will have their turn. There are many to help," she said. "Most of all, it's *imperative* we do this correctly. Records must be filled out completely so they can be returned to Athens." She went behind a table and spoke with another woman who sat with large piles of paper in front of her. The crowd slowly settled down.

He approached one of the people in line, an old man wearing a gray, tattered wool overcoat and black cap, with curiosity. "What is happening?" he asked.

"The children in the capital," the old man explained. "The Red Cross is sending them out of the city to rural areas until the famine ends. They need sponsors." A chill went down Tasso's spine as the old man continued. "Some have gone to relatives, but there are more who have no one. They need food." As the man explained the Red Cross's fostering system, Tasso recalled his conversation with Father Tomas. In that moment he knew God was presenting him with an opportunity to help.

"Where do I sign up?" he asked.

"You may wait in this line," the Red Cross woman said, appearing next to him. "And I will need to see your papers," she said.

Tasso reached into his jacket pocket and handed her his identification. He got in line, with several people ahead of him. After nearly thirty minutes, he reached the front. While he answered several questions, the woman wearing a cap stitched with a cross in red thread filled out several pieces of paper. When the process was completed, she smiled up at him.

"We have a boy," she said. "He is eleven years old. His name is Luka."

A huge smile spread across Tasso's face as he realized the foster boy was the same age as Nikola.

"However," she said, "there is one more thing we need before placing him with you." He put his anticipation on hold as she explained that because of his status as a soldier, the Red Cross required the consent of a secondary foster parent, either his wife or a sibling.

"My wife is in our village. Would my sister-in-law do?" he asked, hoping she would consent. Tasso had already explained his purpose in Sparta and how he expected Nikola to be released soon.

"That would be fine," she answered, "but she must sign this document before we can make this complete."

He took the papers from her and held them in his hand, reading his name at the top and the details below. "Thank you, ma'am," he said.

She added that once the Red Cross received the papers with Maria's signature, and he was ready to return to Vassara, he could pick up the boy. She also told him that Luka was an only child, whose father had been killed in action. There was little more known about the boy's background, just that he had been brought to the government offices in Athens to be placed with a foster family by his mother. Tasso assured the Red Cross worker that he would return the next day with both signatures and reiterated that he would be heading home as soon as Nikola was released from the hospital. Until then, he learned, Luka would wait at the Red Cross facility in Sparta.

Tasso looked down at the slip of paper, reading the boy's age once more. Then he folded the paper and put it in his breast pocket. Walking away from the crowd, he smiled, looked up, and made the sign of the cross. *Thank you, Lord. Thank you for letting me do this.*

But as he continued toward the hospital, doubt crept into his head, and the complexity of the situation became real. *What if Nikola's health takes a turn for the worse? What if we have to stay in Sparta longer? Is it fair to make the foster child wait? How in the world will I explain this to Maria?* Convincing her would not be easy, he thought, but he knew Diamanto would support the idea.

He walked into the medical building with a million concerns on his mind, but before he could say anything, Maria came to him at once. She had been waiting for him anxiously, she said. Her face was glowing with a gigantic grin.

"Good news!" She embraced him. "Nikola is healing well. The doctors say he can continue with crutches on his own now, and as long as he keeps progressing, he can go home soon."

Tasso was overjoyed. "Wonderful! May I see him?" he asked, grateful for the encouraging news.

"Of course! He's tired from the exercises, but he's been asking for you all afternoon." She paused. "How was your trip to town?"

He put his arm around her as they walked. "Let's go see Nikola first. I have plenty of news for you both!"

Tasso was happy to see his nephew sitting up and drawing. He sat with him on the bed, and they made sketches together late into the day. They drew houses and trees, churches and bridges, while Maria looked on. He could see the passion in the boy's expression as he illustrated. Meanwhile, Luka was on Tasso's mind, and he pondered how to explain everything to Maria. He would plead with her if necessary, he thought, hoping her son's recovery might win her over.

When Nikola fell asleep later that evening, Tasso and Maria stepped out into the hallway.

"What is it?" she asked.

"Nothing is wrong," he explained. "I just want to tell you about this morning … When I was in town today, I came across some people from Athens, people from the Red Cross."

"Who are they?" she asked.

He took a breath and continued. "They are here because of the children in Athens." He went on to explain about the food shortage and the system that had been set up to foster children and how he had committed to care for Luka.

"You want to add *another* child to our family during the war? How will he eat? Is he really better off with *us*?" she inquired.

"I don't think you realize how bad things are in Athens," he answered gently.

Maria made a stern face at him before saying, "My sister will think we have lost our minds!"

Tasso's eyes widened. If she were completely against the idea, he thought, she would have reacted with more disapproval. "Leave Diamanto to me," he answered. "I will write to her and explain." He paused and took her hands into his. "Maria, God has blessed this family with an abundance of good fortune. Look at how your son was saved! Many are in need far more than us. If we can help them, perhaps this whole mess is worth something." As Tasso heard his own words, his spirit strengthened, and for the first time, he contemplated the idea that the events of his life were part of a greater plan, one he never could have foreseen.

Maria exhaled and shocked him by answering, "As you wish, Tasso."

At long last, Nikola was ready to return to Vassara. He practiced walking on crutches and, little by little, regained much of his leg's strength.

Tasso was overjoyed at the boy's reaction when he told him about Luka in his room one night before bed.

"I can't wait to meet him!" Nikola said as Maria bent over to kiss her son on the forehead.

"You'd better write that letter to my sister before we show up in the village with another mouth to feed!" Maria warned as she stood upright. Nikola was to be released from the hospital within a few days, and Tasso knew she was right.

He stayed up late to perfect the note he had drafted to Diamanto, rereading it one last time before sending it ahead to Vassara.

My dearest Mandini,

May this note find you and the children well. Kiss them a hundred times for me. Certainly, you are all still celebrating the good news of Nikola's improvement. It is my hope that what I'm about to share with you will also be seen as a blessing in your eyes. As you know from my last letter, my brother remains missing, and the famine in Athens has hit hard the children of our country. Both burdens weigh so heavily on me, despite the good news of our nephew's recovery. I have worked to keep my faith strong, and I pray God will provide resolution to all of our uncertainties. The answers sometimes are not what we expect, as I learned when I encountered the Red Cross in Sparta. They came to town to ask families to temporarily foster Athenian children, hoping to relocate them in rural parts of the country so that they may be saved from starvation. Mandini, I felt as if God was speaking directly to me that day. Even with all of our troubles, we must help those in greater need. I had no hesitation because I know you have a generous heart. Surely, the burden of caring for the children falls on you. However, I pray you approve my decision to help a boy in need. His name is Luka. He is from Halandri, just outside Athens. His father was killed in the war, and his mother placed him with the Red Cross for fear he would starve to death. Maria has agreed to help with the boy, so Luka will be in the care of both our families. I know this is unexpected and that once my leg heals, I must leave again, but even with food stretched for our own children, I know we can stretch even further to save a child. I can't do anything to save my brother, but perhaps this was the Lord's plan, to heal Nikola so that we may heal someone else.

Please do not be cross with me. Help me to welcome Luka into our family for this short time. He is the same age as Nikola, and you would be amazed at how the promise of a new friend has excited our nephew. We will find a way to care for all of them, I promise.

Take care of yourself, my darling, and with the blessings of God, I will see you shortly in Vassara.

Love to you always,
Your Tasso

After Nikola's much-anticipated discharge from the hospital, Tasso helped his nephew navigate down the stairs of the medical building with crutches. The boy was still slightly pale, but his joviality began to return, and when he smiled, Tasso's whole world seemed right. He set the boy comfortably in the back of the carriage while Maria sat in the front seat. There were blankets spread all over to make the boys comfortable. As he climbed into the driver's side, he thought of Petro's generosity for lending the carriage. Without it, he didn't know how he would have managed. They headed straight from the hospital to meet Luka. The children's orphanage was not far from the center of Sparta.

Tasso parked the carriage and got out at the white building that matched the address on his slip of paper with Luka's name. A Red Cross banner hung across the archway of the building. Large stone steps led up to a pair of tall, wooden double doors. He showed his identification to an elderly lady who sat outside the building. She told him to wait as she stepped inside. His heart beat fast, and his hands felt clammy. Returning a few minutes later with a paper for him to sign, the lady showed him inside, where he confirmed the arrangements. While the woman checked the paper, Tasso grew more nervous.

He heard Luka's name called out and looked down a narrow hallway.

A young boy came forward, holding a small green bag. Surely, he thought, the boy's nerves were worse than his. He was almost the same height as Nikola, with pin-straight blonde hair. But he was drastically thin, with large, sad blue eyes and sunken cheeks. He wore only a torn gray short-sleeved shirt and pants a few inches too short. Tasso noticed the ragged condition of his shoes with split soles. The boy looked up at him, seeming afraid. His mouth opened as if to say something, but no words came out.

Tasso squatted down to meet his eyes. He held out his hand and smiled. "You must be Luka. Hello. I am Tasso. I'm here to bring you to stay with me and my family in Vassara for a while. Would that be all right with you?" He made a special effort to speak gently and kept his large hand stretched out.

The boy continued to look at him, moving his head slowly as if to measure Tasso's size with his eyes. "Are you …" The boy cleared his throat. "Aren't you … a soldier?" he asked.

"Yes, I am." Tasso smiled. "I've come back from Albania, and now I'm home for a while to heal my leg and help my family. Would you like to stay with us?"

Luka slowly started to form a smile. "Yes, please."

"Wonderful! Come and meet my nephew Nikola." Tasso stood up, and they started out the doors together and walked down the steps in front of the building. "He has just been released from the hospital," Tasso continued. "You are both the same age, I think." Tasso turned to point toward the carriage, where Nikola was sitting up with blankets propping up his bad leg, waving to the boy.

"Hello, Luka!" Nikola shouted.

Luka smiled and looked down to his feet and then up to Tasso. The boy softly asked, "He had polio, right? Mrs. Anton from the Red Cross told me." There was a pause. "I'm glad he's okay. I prayed for him."

Tasso got choked up for a moment before answering, "Thank you." He stroked the hair on Luka's head and put his hand on the boy's shoulder as they walked toward the carriage. "He is much better now. You will also meet my children, George and Elaine, who are close to your age. We have a little one named Maria. Nikola also has two brothers and a sister." Tasso chuckled. "There will be plenty of children for you to play with in Vassara."

"I have no brothers or sisters," said the boy.

Tasso helped Luka climb into the carriage and introduced him to Nikola and Maria. Luka moved slowly, showing caution for Nikola's outstretched leg. Maria held out her hand to the boy and then kissed Luka on both cheeks, offering him dried fruit as he sat down. Tasso walked to the front of the carriage and untied the donkeys before climbing into his seat. Within moments, he heard the two boys in the back laughing.

As he navigated the carriage down the city street and headed for the road out of town, Maria touched his arm. "I believe you came to Sparta to save *two* boys, Tasso."

He steered down the street, looking back again at the smiling boys. Nikola was showing Luka his crutches.

Nikola loved being treated like a celebrity when he returned to Vassara and didn't mind sharing some of the attention with Luka. His uncle Tasso had told him to be very conscientious of the boy's feelings, pointing out also that Luka was probably missing his mother in Athens.

"Just make sure you're always kind to him. He is delicate in spirit, as you are delicate in your recovering body. I pray both of you heal and grow into happy, healthy young men." His uncle's words replayed in his mind often.

"I understand, Uncle," Nikola had promised him. "I will make him feel at home here."

What Nikola wasn't prepared for were the constant questions villagers asked about his health and his new friend.

"Look!" he said, picking up his crutches to show his improved mobility to them.

Old ladies put pieces of hard candy into his hand and brought clothing for Luka. A few other Athenian children arrived in Vassara as well, but most of them were toddlers brought to distant relatives. Nikola loved that he and Luka were so popular.

Even more, Nikola appreciated Luka's loyalty as he sat at Nikola's bedside whenever he was forced to rest his leg, either out of pain or at his mother's insistence. On account of such devotion, the Athenian boy became like another brother to Nikola. They shared everything, and while his other brothers helped their mother with chores, Nikola had found a soul mate just the right age. He hadn't been this happy since before his onset of polio.

A few weeks after their arrival, while Nikola and Luka sat under a shaded tree on a wooden bench in the town center, a man on a wagon arrived. He had several large sacks of papers. The stranger got out of the wagon and began nailing the papers on the large trees that surrounded Mr. Natakos's café. Villagers immediately stopped what they were doing and walked over to look at the notices. Nikola tried to get up quickly too but dropped one of his crutches.

"I'll go," Luka said, motioning for him to stay where he was. Nikola sat back down and watched his friend run over to the tree. He wished he had full command of his crutches, but he wasn't able to move quickly. He couldn't wait to be free of them. He looked on as Luka stood in front of the notice and read the paper out loud for the elders to hear, several of whom had never learned to read.

After the man on the wagon left the square and headed up the road leading to the neighboring village of Verroia, Nikola tried to listen closely to what Luka was saying. His friend spoke in a loud voice, announcing that the notice came from the Greek government. It was an order for firearms to be turned over to the authorities. "With the war efforts escalating, the Greek government demands any and all guns," Luka read aloud. Not to do so would be against the law, he went on to say. "Violators will be punished." Nikola was stunned by the news and thought instantly of his uncle's guns.

As soon as Luka returned to the bench, Nikola said, "We have to tell my uncle right away!"

They went to his uncle's house as quickly as possible. Nikola even tried to skip along the road with his crutches but lost his balance a few times and was forced to slow down. They burst through the kitchen door and saw his aunt Diamanto standing over a fireplace, cooking greens.

"Where's Uncle Tasso?" he panted urgently.

"Out back chopping wood. Are you all right?" she asked, turning to them.

"The government wants everyone's guns!" he told her. Nikola saw the expression on his aunt's face change. She motioned for his grandmother Georgia to watch the food while she went with the boys.

"Tasso?" she called out.

"Over here," he replied. They followed her around to the back of the house.

Luka spoke slowly, recounting all the details of the notice. Nikola watched his uncle make the same face as his aunt. As Tasso put down his axe, Nikola knew his uncle was thinking of the two prized firearms that had been passed down from his family in Longastra. The pair of hunting rifles was worth far more than money—that was certain. But before Nikola had a chance to say anything, his uncle went into the house.

His aunt had just summoned them inside her kitchen to wash up when around the corner came Fofo, his younger sister. She said she had been sent by their mother to fetch Luka. Maria needed help with something Nikola couldn't do on account of his leg. While Luka set off with Fofo, Nikola cleaned his hands and proceeded upstairs to find his uncle. Taking each stair carefully with his crutches in tow, he was determined to see him.

He breathed heavily, panting from the exertion, as he climbed the stairs with difficulty. Entering the upstairs, he saw his uncle standing in the bedroom near the fireplace, holding two rifles, one in each hand. Tasso turned around and looked at him in earnest.

"We can't let these go, Nikola," he said. "They've been in my family for decades. Above all, we need them for protection. They're the only way we can defend your mama, your aunt Diamanto, and you children." Tasso's tone was serious.

Nikola stood speechless as he watched his uncle hold the guns. His heart beat fast.

"You understand what I'm telling you?" Tasso asked him.

"Yes, Uncle," he replied, not exactly sure. Wanting to appear mature, he straightened his posture on the crutches with a serious expression.

Frozen where he stood, Nikola watched as Tasso walked around the upstairs of the house and entered each room. He knocked on almost all the walls, putting his ears to the plaster. It was then that Nikola realized his uncle was trying to find a place to hide the firearms. In the second bedroom, Tasso knocked repeatedly on what he said was a "soft" wall and explained the plan to bury the guns within the walls of the home.

"That way, when the war is over, I can retrieve them," his uncle said to him. "But if something happens to me, Nikola, you must remember to tell your aunt Diamanto where they are hidden. Understand?"

"Yes, Uncle," he said, fighting back the horrid thought that something might happen to his uncle.

Tasso said that if anyone asked about the guns, he should say they were with Tasso's relatives in Longastra. Within an hour, and with only a small amount of Nikola's help, Tasso opened the wall and placed both rifles, wrapped in a tattered red and gray striped blanket, inside the hole with ammunition.

"Go downstairs now and tell everyone I am resting," Tasso said to him.

"Yes, Uncle." He left the room just as Tasso started to close the wall. As he descended the staircase with care, he thought he comprehended the severity of the secret.

Several hours later, Tasso headed downstairs. He was still shaking inside, questioning his decision to hide the guns. Was this the best place? He hoped he hadn't scared his nephew. He thanked his wife for the quiet time. She gave him a funny look, surely having heard the banging and thumping of plaster, but she never questioned him.

Late that night, he sat in the kitchen, having tea with Diamanto, while Georgia was upstairs putting the children to bed. There was a fast knock at the door. Diamanto immediately looked at him with concern.

"Uncle Tasso?" Nikola said, softly opening the door.

Surprised to see him, he asked, "Why aren't you asleep?"

"I'm so sorry! Please, Uncle, please forgive me!" The boy limped over, buried his head in his uncle's stomach, and threw his crutch to the floor. Weeping, he wrapped his arms around Tasso's waist.

"What is it, Nikola? What's the matter?" he asked.

"I … I told someone," the boy sobbed.

Tasso felt the blood drain from his face. Stunned, he grabbed Nikola by the arms, squatting down to look his nephew in the eye. "Who, Nikola? Who did you tell?" he asked urgently.

"I told Luka," Nikola sobbed. "We were playing behind the church. No one was around."

And then Luka slowly appeared from outside and stepped into the doorway where Tasso could see him. The boy had been hiding outside. Seeing the fear on Luka's face, Tasso let out a large exhale.

"Come here, Luka. Do not be afraid," he instructed.

Both boys were trembling, and Nikola would not lift his head.

"Luka," he said, "I need to ask you a special favor." He paused to collect himself, trying to speak as kindly as possible to the foster boy, not wanting to undo the good that had been done since the boy's arrival. Although he was relieved that only the boys knew, he still had to worry about someone overhearing the information.

"Anything," Luka said. "I'll do anything."

Tasso forced a smile. "I know," he said, "and I know you're a good boy, as you are part of our family."

The boy's face seemed to relax.

Tasso continued. "I want both of you to go to Nikola's house for a while. Stay there and say nothing to anyone about this." He looked at his wife.

Diamanto nodded. "I will walk the boys over," she offered.

"Thank you, Mandini," he answered.

"Luka, you are not to tell *anyone* about what Nikola shared with you." He placed his hand on Luka's shoulder.

"I will never speak a word of it. I promise." The young boy started to compose himself.

"I believe you. I know you understand how important my request is. Thank you for your obedience. Now go, both of you, while I take care of this." He motioned for the boys to leave, and they did. But just before exiting the doorway, Nikola stopped and turned back.

"Uncle Tasso?" he mumbled through tears. "I'm so, so sorry. I beg your forgiveness. Please don't hate me. Please, Uncle Tasso. I know I was wrong. Please don't hate me."

Tasso opened his arms, and Nikola fell into his chest, blubbering. He hadn't planned to talk with his nephew until later about what it meant to trust each other, but from the look on the boy's face, the talk couldn't wait. Luka stood outside waiting with his head down.

"Come closer, Luka," he said, opening his arms to hold both boys together. "Boys, if we don't have trust in our family, we have nothing." He paused and then lifted Nikola's chin to look the boy in the eyes. "I could never hate you. You know better than to say such a thing. You made a mistake today, one that I don't think you'll ever make again. Am I right?"

"Yes. Yes, Uncle Tasso. I will never break anyone's trust again, I promise."

"Good. Now go with Luka and don't talk about this to anyone."

The boys left holding Diamanto's hands. As the door closed behind them, Tasso rubbed his chin, pondering the next step. He had to get the guns out of the house immediately, so there was no other choice but to open the wall and remove them. The last thing he wanted was to redo the job, but with determination and a few small glasses of wine, Tasso began again with all the strength and speed he could muster. Packing the rifles and ammunition into a satchel, he resurfaced the wall late into the night, trying his best to make the area appear undisturbed.

Drinking the last sip, he put the empty glass upside down on the table beside him and headed out of the house with his satchel, walking alone through the dark, cold streets of Vassara. No one would see him at this late hour. When Tasso returned, he was empty-handed.

Chapter Eleven

Tasso stood next to Petro on a high ridge overlooking his friend's field. Sunset approached, and the once bright, blaring sun conceded through muted tones of pink in a transforming sky. Petro's goats settled quietly behind a fence, gathered around a water trough. They appeared indifferent to the small plane flying overhead. Before Tasso could get a better look, the plane vanished behind a high green hill. Petro shook his head while a cold chill ran down Tasso's spine.

"That's the second plane this week," moaned Petro.

"We need to prepare ourselves," Tasso added, reflecting on a conversation he'd had with a group of old men in the town square that morning, warning them to hide their valuables. They had discussed escape possibilities, and he had helped strategize with families that had daughters.

"I thought you'd scare them with your warnings today, but you're right," said Petro. "They need to be ready. I've hidden some grain in the hills—my cousin's idea. He said people in his village buried food in case of a raid. It's the demand for guns that changed everything. No wonder everyone seems uneasy." He leaned in and lowered his voice. "I would *never* give my guns to the government." Petro shook his head once more.

"I agree, Petro. I agree," Tasso answered.

"See you at church tomorrow, friend," Petro said as little Kosma came from behind and hugged his father at the knees.

The next day, Tasso stepped out the door to leave for church with his family and noticed several Vassareans carrying satchels.

When they passed his doorway, he asked, "What are you bringing with you?"

"I am hiding my grandparents' wedding rings," an old woman replied.

She held up a small cloth bag. "If I put them in the church, the Germans won't get them."

"I'm hiding a few gold coins that my brother sent me from America," added another older gentleman.

Tasso stopped in surprise. What were they thinking? He looked at the group holding bundles of various sizes, some with determined expressions.

"No!" he objected. "St. George is *not* the place!" His voice was urgent. "Our churches are not sacred to the Nazis!"

Before he could continue, the woman with the gold wedding bands argued, "But surely they won't steal from the house of God!"

He took a deep breath and turned to Diamanto, who came up behind him wearing her Sunday dress of pink flowers against an off-white background. Georgia and Kotso stood close. Diamanto gave him a look he knew as a warning to be cautious, and Kotso moved past his wife and daughter, stepping into the street next to Tasso.

"Take the children ahead, Diamanto," Tasso said to his wife. She nodded and motioned for them to come with her.

George protested. "Mama, I want to hear what Baba has to say!"

"George, come! Baba will meet us at church. Help me light candles," she said, directing him away.

He nodded to his son, and the boy turned to walk with his sisters, mother, and grandmother. Kotso followed slowly behind.

Tasso turned back to the crowd. "Have we forgotten what our ancestors went through with the Persians? They no more respect the church and its sanctity than the lives of women and children! Don't you see? This is why we have made escape plans for our young girls and mothers." He became increasingly angry as he spoke. Beads of sweat gathered around his temple, and the white shirt underneath his suit coat grew damp.

"This church," he continued, pointing to St. George, "and all the others like it will be the first place they ransack. Take your valuables home and put them elsewhere. Some of you have hidden your grain, your guns ..." He dared mention the firearms while knowing he had done the same. A few heads in the crowd looked down as he spoke. "I don't pass judgment on what you do, but *please* don't leave your things in the church! They'll be the first things stolen." He lowered his voice, hoping his plea was understood.

There was some mumbling among the group, and a few started to nod their heads. He saw a couple of old women put their small bags back into their pockets. He closed the door to the house behind him to leave for church.

As Tasso turned his back, one old man called out, "I don't care what he says. These are *my* things, and I will do with them what I please!"

Tasso heard the comment but didn't answer. He had offered his opinion, and whether or not the Vassareans took his advice was their decision. But the ugly memories of war invaded his memory as he continued up the path. Scenes of men dying at the battlefront kept replaying in his head. He imagined the villagers would learn firsthand the trials of war. An ominous weight of doom hovered over him, and he found it hard to feel optimistic about anything.

As he approached the bell tower, he knew only the Divine Liturgy would soften his heart. When he reached St. George's main door, Kotso was there waiting for him. The old man had a sad expression.

"I realize they need you, Tasso," Kotso said to him, "but I think the time has come for you to worry about your own family. Let these villagers take care of themselves."

He was surprised by his father-in-law's words but understood the old man's frustration.

"You've done so much for them," Kotso continued. "They have escape plans; they've hidden their valuables … safely now, because of you." He paused and reached up to Tasso's shoulder, looking him in the eye. "One man cannot defend this entire village. If the Germans find you here, son, they'll kill you first."

Tasso looked at Kotso's cloudy eyes. "What are you saying?" he asked.

The old man had the most sincere expression. "Ever since you told me about your visit to Magoula, I've started to think that perhaps you should go there … now."

Tasso didn't know what to think.

"Your leg is healing. It won't be long before you're called back. Go to Magoula. Be near the city. That's where you belong. It's safer. In the meantime, enjoy your family, and when you have to leave, my daughter and the children will have the house and, hopefully, the fields," he explained.

"But there's still work to be done," Tasso said. "You don't think the children and Diamanto are better off in Vassara?"

The old man remained quiet for a moment. "I'm afraid of what will happen if the Germans find you here." Then he looked away, and at once, Tasso's heavy heart sank deeper into his chest. Although he knew the old man made sense, he didn't know what to do.

Kotso persisted. "You said you got a good look at the house. Finish it—the coop, the floors, the windows and doors. Make it as secure as you can." The old man's voice started to crack. "Perhaps you can plant those lemon and orange trees if there is time."

With his comment about the trees, Tasso knew his father-in-law was trying to persuade with whatever means possible. The beloved orchards were Tasso's soft spot, and the old man knew it. But he appreciated his father in-law's gentleness, void of a dictatorial tone. He respected that Kotso wanted the best for his daughter and grandchildren.

"This is a big decision," Tasso answered. "How can I take Diamanto away from her sister, and the children from their cousins?" he asked.

Kotso didn't hesitate before responding. "If you don't, you will be killed here. At least if you leave, there's a chance for you." With that, he turned away, ending the debate.

Tasso observed the steeple of St. George. "Let's go to church and pray," he offered. "The answers will come to us."

Kotso followed him inside the narthex. While his father-in-law greeted some elders, Tasso lit a single, thin, yellow beeswax candle and stood it upright within a tray of white sand next to three tall icons. Kotso put a few coins in the basket, and Tasso approached the icon of the Virgin Mary, praying for the protection of both the village and his family. He asked for guidance as well, hoping to decide his next move wisely.

Throughout the liturgy, Tasso pondered the old man's plea. The truth was he had been considering the same thoughts ever since visiting Magoula. But hearing someone else suggest it strengthened his belief that leaving Vassara was the right thing to do. He resolved during Holy Communion to present the idea to Diamanto.

Later that day, Tasso took out the plans he had drawn for the Magoula home. They had been sitting inside a chest in the upstairs bedroom. He had placed them there for safekeeping and hadn't looked at them since before Albania. Just holding the sketches and reading his own notes along the side margins excited him. Recalculating the number of trees the land could support and recalling what he had seen on his recent visit, Tasso confirmed enough space for 350 trees in an area that, with the help of the Sanos boy's friends, he hoped to clear and prepare. Perhaps he might get to those trees, he thought.

As he ran his finger across the page, looking at the other marked-off areas set aside for a chicken coop and crops, a half smile returned to his face. The end result would be a self-sustaining paradise with Sparta's topography, a farmer's dream, he thought: lush with rich earth, plenty of sun year round, and adequate rainfall.

Diamanto entered the room with a tray, bringing him a late-afternoon coffee in a small china demitasse cup. The ornate gold décor around the rim of the cup depicted ships sailing in the ocean. He appreciated that his wife placed the cup and saucer safely away from his papers along with a tall glass of water.

"Thank you." He looked up at his wife and wrapped his arm around her waist.

She moved in close. "I thought you would need this. You've been up here for a while. What are you looking at?" she asked as she glanced over the papers. "Ahhh," she said before he could answer. "I see you've been talking to my father."

"You *know* about his idea?" As the words came out, he half-laughed to himself, reminded once more of the bond between father and daughter, one that had always been strong. Of course she already knew of Kotso's plan.

"He told me that he thinks we should go to Magoula. I know he is right, but I would be so sad to leave them," she said as he took his first sip of the hot coffee and placed the small cup back down on its saucer. His large fingers could barely fit through the delicate cup's handle.

"That's what I told him," he said, pausing as a fresh thought came to his head, one he knew would ease her heart and satisfy him as well. "Diamanto, what if your parents came *with* us to Magoula?"

Diamanto's eyes opened wide, and he could see the idea pleased her.

"They could close up the house here and come as well. Lord knows we could use the extra help getting the house ready," he suggested.

"Oh, Tasso, that would be wonderful!" she answered softly.

When her look suddenly changed, he inquired, "What is it?"

"What about Luka?" she asked. "We can't separate the boys."

"No. They've become too close," he agreed, realizing the additional complexities involved. "Let's talk to Maria and your parents. You know your sister would never leave Vassara to live somewhere else, so perhaps Luka should stay here with her."

"She's bound to this place more than any of us. But she won't want her son to lose his best friend." Diamanto paused. "I believe that boy is healing Nikola's spirits."

"Let me talk to her," he said.

As Tasso expected, Maria was more disappointed about losing her sister and parents than concerned about caring for Luka. Brining home the boy from Athens had turned out to be a blessing, she explained the next day as they all discussed the matter in Maria's kitchen.

"No reservations?" Tasso asked once more, wanting to be sure his sister-in-law was satisfied with the idea.

"None," Maria said, wiping her eyes with a white kerchief.

Diamanto sat next to her sister with an arm around her plump shoulder.

"He has such a sweet demeanor and has been a huge help around here, especially with Nikola." She broke down. "But I worry for you," she cried into Diamanto's arms. "You will be left without your villagers in a place unfamiliar to you. What will happen when Tasso has to leave?" Maria looked at Tasso, and he instantly felt a punch of guilt in his abdomen.

"I will have Mother and Father as my support," Diamanto answered. The optimism in her voice impressed him. "You worry about yourself and the children and your husband, that he may return safely too."

Tasso complimented his wife's strength with a nod and smile while she held Maria.

"I will miss you terribly," Maria said as she sat up from Diamanto's embrace, "but if you can be strong, then perhaps I can do the same."

Tasso smiled at his sister-in-law. "Lord, let us all reunite soon."

The family's departure from Vassara early the following week was a sad day. Villagers gathered outside their home, and although they wished him well, Tasso wondered if they thought he was abandoning them. A small group of old ladies stood together with solemn faces, along with Maria's daughter Fofo, who had always been close to Diamanto. Kotso and Georgia held Maria while Fofo told her aunt over and over how much she would miss her. Nikola stood on crutches next to Luka as tears ran down both their faces. Tasso knew how much the boys would miss him, and he felt the same.

He was glad he had taken Luka aside with Diamanto days earlier and explained to the orphan that he didn't want to separate him from Nikola. Tasso was amazed at the boy's resilience and ability to handle change; it seemed he was used to goodbyes and had been forced to deal with heartbreak more than the average child. Nikola was more emotional, as Tasso expected, and made his uncle promise to return to Vassara as soon as possible. It was hard for him to say goodbye to his nephew, but seeing him in better health gave Tasso hope for the future. Watching his wife leave her relatives was also difficult. At last, it was time to go.

"We are all packed up," he told Diamanto. He turned to Petro, thanking him for once again allowing him to borrow his carriage. They checked the bundles and tightened all the straps. "So," he said to his friend, "Father Tomas will return this carriage next week when he's in Sparta, right?" Tasso asked.

"Exactly," Petro said. "Be safe, my friend."

"I will," he said.

"Petro, you are a good man," Diamanto added.

"Good luck and God be with you!" Petro said to them. The same was heard from many as they climbed in and waved a final goodbye. Tasso looked back at Diamanto, who sat weeping while Elaine, George, Maria, Kotso, and Georgia settled in. Kotso kept waving as the carriage pulled away. Georgia and Diamanto cried. He looked ahead and out toward the blue sky and rewrapped the leather strap around his palm to make the grip tighter.

Sooner than anticipated, they arrived in Magoula, where it didn't take long for the dormant house to revive with activity. The children ran around, squealing with excitement, while he was eager to review the house's condition and show everyone around.

Georgia seemed amazed as she complimented his work. "I've never seen a kitchen so big!" she said.

"Thank you. I'm hoping to make this place comfortable as soon as possible. I just need to arrange some help," he answered. He took his in-laws up the stone staircase that led to the large balcony and showed them the beautiful view of Taygetos that he loved so much.

"This view is breathtaking," said Georgia.

"Well done, Tasso," said Kotso.

"There's still some work in here," he said, pointing to the door leading to the inside of the upstairs, "so be careful as we walk. I want to show you the bedrooms and the fireplace."

He held open the door for them to enter the hallway that led to three bedrooms. "Most of the major projects are done in here," he explained just outside the front bedroom, "except for this!" Tasso pointed to a portion of the room's floor that remained unfinished and was open to the level below.

He added, "I pondered building an inside staircase, but there wasn't enough time to do it right, so I was forced to block off the area."

"Oh my!" said Georgia.

"We'll keep the children out of here and block this off until this section is complete," Kotso said.

Tasso agreed and took them all down the hallway to show them the rest.

Over the next few days, Tasso watched happily as his family members settled into the house, making themselves at home. In addition to Panouli Sanos and his friends, Tasso asked around locally to find men who were looking for work. Most were older or too young for the war, like Panouli, but every extra set of hands made a difference. He planned to offer them food and shelter and what money he could spare for their help working in his fields, planting crops, and assisting with the house. With the summer months beginning and the children free from lessons, he was glad they could hold off on signing up George and Elaine for school in Magoula.

Georgia, Diamanto, Elaine, and George kept busy dusting off the interior and unpacking what they had brought from Vassara. Together with his father-in-law, Tasso went room to room, assessing the roof, flooring, fireplace, and windows.

One project Tasso wanted to complete sooner rather than later was a chicken coop that stood just outside the kitchen door. Its completion was a priority so that they could have both eggs and chickens. Tasso spent just under a week, with George by his side, putting final touches on the building. Diamanto was thrilled at the location and told him she had dreamed of collecting eggs right beside a place to cook. The coop was long and narrow, but with a lower ceiling just tall enough for him to stand inside. When it was finished, he bartered with a nearby farmer to fill the coop with the family's first flock of chickens. In return, he gave the farmer leftover lumber.

Tasso also made time to revisit the medical facility in Sparta for his leg. Happy to see the infection clearing up, the doctor warned him to keep the area clean and not overwork himself. He also advised that Tasso could present himself for active duty in less than a month. Hearing the news made Tasso both happy and stressed; his time at home was running out. Therefore, he rose early each day with renewed purpose and worked with little rest before the sky turned black.

In the meantime, he had a separate project unrelated to securing the home. He wanted to set up a large wardrobe he had purchased over a year ago as a gift for Diamanto. He hoped the beautiful piece of furniture would help her feel at home. Having stored it for safekeeping, Tasso was determined to get the piece into the room and add the legs and door as well as a top decorative piece that would make the wardrobe ready to use. The tall, single-door chest had carved leaves that made a beautiful pattern in the wood. There was little other furniture in the home other than beds and a few tables, so he was certain this would make her happy.

The wardrobe required its final touches to be added inside the upstairs bedroom because the chest stood taller than the frame of the door once its legs were added and the top piece was in place. It was an enormous piece of furniture, and Tasso needed both the Sanos boy and two of the boy's friends to assist in the process. Once the assembly was finished, they placed it adjacent to the fireplace, and Tasso admired the piece. He opened the wardrobe's door and showed the boys the full-length mirror inside. There were shelves and a bar across the top for hanging garments, with ample space to accommodate his long clothing as well as his wife's items. He smiled with a heart full of pride for the beautiful centerpiece of their bedroom.

While final details of the home were addressed, new vegetable plantings in the garden began to take root and, after several weeks, showed promise. He was cautiously optimistic, hoping the self-sustaining farm could provide his family with food in the days ahead. As the twinge in his leg disappeared, he knew he'd be leaving soon and hung on to the relief that they were settled in Magoula. With only the upstairs bedroom floor needing repair, he marked the completion of his home by climbing the roof and etching his name, "Anastasios Stamatopoulos," into the last shingle placed atop his dream home.

A little over a month after their arrival, as the family gathered for a midday meal under the shade in the courtyard one afternoon, a young Greek soldier not much older than the Sanos boy appeared at their gate. The boy asked for him by name. Tasso came forward to receive the papers as the soldier put two large envelopes between the metal bars.

"Messages for you, sir," the young boy in uniform said.

Tasso opened the first envelope and felt life leave his body as he read confirmation that his brother had been captured and taken out of the country along with a large group of Greek prisoners. He gasped at the news and put his hand to his chest.

"What is it, Tasso?" Diamanto asked.

Consumed by the dreadful information, Tasso's heart was unmoved when he opened the second envelope and saw that its contents instructed him to appear the following day in Sparta at military headquarters. His orders had come through with a promotion.

"Captain?" he said softly, his mind still on Dimitri.

"Yes, sir!" replied the young soldier. Tasso turned around to Diamanto, who had stood up from her chair. The color was gone from her face.

"What is it, my dear?" she asked.

Clearing a sob from his throat, he replied, "The army has confirmed Dimitri has been taken prisoner, and I am to report at once. They have made me captain."

Anastasios Stamatopoulos

Diamanto Laskari

Kostandinos (Kotso) Laskari, Diamanto's father

Diamanto's mother, Georgia Laskari

Tasso and Diamanto by Sparta's fountain

Tasso and Diamanto's engagement photograph

Tasso and Diamanto on their wedding day

Elaine, George, and Maria on the balcony stairs at the Magoula house

Sisters Diamanto (left) and Maria (right) with their father Kotso (center), along with Elaine (front left), George (back left), Fofo (back right), and Yianni (front right)

Kotso and Georgia (center) with their grandchildren Elaine (left), George (front center), and Maria (front right). In the back: Diamanto and unidentified woman.

The hand painted icon that was given to Kotso Laskari in the 1800s.

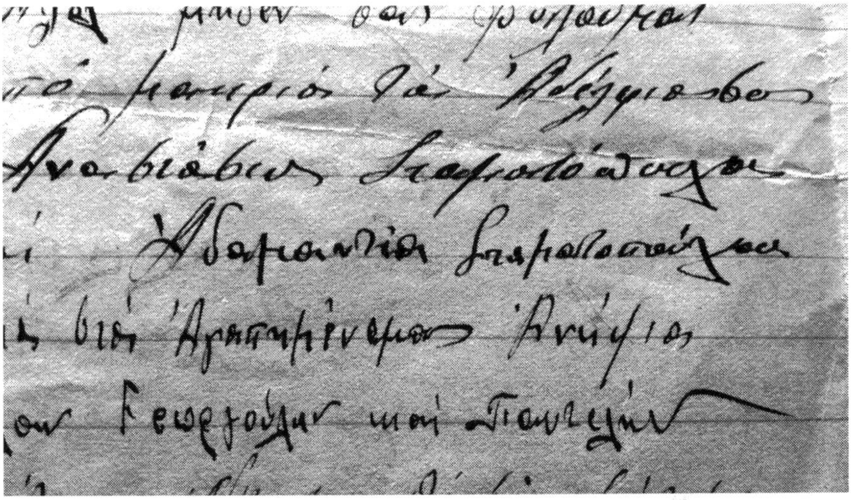

Tasso's letter to his sister in law Pota in Montana, describing the wedding between he and Diamanto.

A certificate presented to Diamanto Stamatopoulos after Tasso's death, commemorating the sacrifice of his life for his country.

ΙΠΛΩΜΑ

Ο ΟΡΚΟΣ ΤΩΝ ΕΛΛΗΝΩΝ

Ὁρκίζομαι στὴ φλόγα τῶν Ὁμήρων,
Ὁρκίζομαι στὴν ἄσβυστην Ἑλλάδα
τοῦ λόγου, τῆς ἰδέας καὶ τῶν ὀνείρων,
Ὁρκίζομαι στὸ φῶς καὶ τὴν ὑγεία
στὴ πίστη τῶν πατέρων τὴν ἁγία,
Ὁρκίζομαι, Γῆ θεία τῆς Ρωμηοσύνης,
στ' ἀρχαῖα σου καὶ τὰ νέα σου παλληκάρια,
Φωκάδες, Καραϊσκάκηδες, Λεωνίδες,
ἢ τὴν ἀσπίδα ἢ στὴν ἀσπίδα ἐπάνω
Ὁρκίζομαι σ' ἐσὲ τοὺς Διγενῆδες
ποὺ γεννᾷς. Θὰ νικήσω ἢ θὰ πεθάνω.

Words from the certificate commemorating Tasso's sacrifice for Greece.

Chapter Twelve

On the morning of his departure, Tasso took one last look at his nearly completed dream house. Wearing a patched-up army jacket, he rested his large hands at his thick leather belt, inspecting the property from one end to the other in a final assessment. His eyes wandered up and down, taking a mental photograph of his project. He wanted to remember every detail of the property because these images would sustain him.

Looking at the fields to the left, he was glad the corn crops were planted, as well as the beans. This would provide for his family, he thought, as would the spinach, potatoes, and tomatoes that were well on their way to a good harvest. Bright bean sprouts with tiny leaves and tomato plants that had begun climbing on wooden stakes offered optimism to his heavy heart. More than before, Tasso was glad Kotso and Georgia were there to provide support for his wife as he returned to war. Postponing the planting of lemon and orange trees had been the correct decision, but he wished they were already taking root like the vegetables. He and Diamanto had agreed that the crops had to be planted first in order to feed everyone.

In the meantime, the orchards he dreamed of would have to wait. Gazing across the courtyard to the property set aside for trees, he breathed a heavy sigh, thankful the land had finally been cleared. For five long days, he had toiled with determination, cutting the brush while removing the mature rooted weeds and thorns that littered the land. At last, the ground stood clean as a prairie, pure and perfect. The impatient earth called to his soul while an aching to live peacefully with his wife and children made him clench the straps of his army satchel. He looked to the left, imagining row after row of mature lemon and orange trees, the beautiful colored fruit shining in the morning sun. He pictured Elaine, George, and little Maria running through countless rows of trees, playing catch with a lemon, and stopping under the cool shade of the mature trees to share a ripened orange. This was all he wanted. Was he asking so much? Over his right arm, however, hung the reality of a soldier's bag, heavy with burden and uncertainty. Would the actuality on the right side of his body allow for the dream on the left? Only time could tell.

Looking forward at the large gate and upward at the balcony on the second level, he exhaled again. The areas with new windows and doors stood shiny and pristine. From the outside, the home appeared sparkling and complete. Inside, however, the home lacked final points of completion, which he had to accept. Dirt floors remained in the lower level, waiting for him to lay wood planks, and the floor upstairs was only half in place, still leaving the gaping hole.

The time for farewells arrived. The children came down from the upstairs, and when Diamanto entered the courtyard with her parents, he could see that she had been crying. As Diamanto stood next to her parents, her head down with a kerchief to her face, Tasso embraced Kotso and Georgia. His in-laws bade him farewell and then stayed back in the courtyard, allowing Tasso to be alone with wife and children. Elaine's eyes were red, and George was quiet while Maria played with her doll, innocently unaware. He smiled at her, fighting back his own tears. They followed him like little ducklings toward the gate. He worked hard not to break down in front of them.

He and Diamanto exchanged few words as they walked out the gate together and down the dirt road. George and Maria hung onto his legs like monkeys on a tree while he held the hands of Elaine and his wife. Kotso and Georgia waved at the gate while he strolled with his family down the road toward the main street, where he would disappear from sight for God knows how long.

He stopped just before the end of the road and kissed each one of his children several times, all over their faces and heads, telling the two older ones to help their mama and look out for one another. Diamanto kept silent as tears streamed down her reddened cheeks. Then he turned to her and placed his large hands on her shoulders.

"The crops will give you adequate food." He talked to his wife uneasily at first, awkwardly going over a checklist of things, trying not to give in to the crescendo of emotions building in his heart.

Diamanto nodded but said nothing. She just cried.

"The beans are almost ready for picking, and soon the first tomatoes will be red." As he continued, she wept more. He exhaled deeply. Trying to sound brave for his wife and cupping her face with gentle palms, he said, "You can do this. I know you can." His reassuring tone was filled with confidence in his wife. She closed her eyes as another gush of tears fell.

She murmured back, "I love you, I love you, I love you," and nothing more, but he needed nothing else.

"May God reunite us again, my Mandini. I love you more than my heart can hold." He kissed her lips and then her forehead, before looking intensely into her eyes. Wishing he could transfer strength from his spirit to hers, he gave her a long, loving look of endearment before hugging the children again. George held on to his neck with a tight grip. He kissed each of them on the forehead and made the sign of the cross over their heads before turning away.

"We love you, Baba!" cried Elaine.

"Love you!" yelled Maria as she hung on to Diamanto's apron.

"I love you too!" he answered, looking back only once to wave to his family, unable to hide his emotions. Readjusting his heavy army bag on his shoulder, he turned down the main street that led into town, dreading his days to come in service once more. By foot he headed into Sparta, a quick fifteen-minute walk of freedom that would end where he was to report for duty at the army offices and receive his orders. As he walked, he prayed for his family, not for himself.

Several months had passed since her husband left. Diamanto wasn't sure how she had managed to hold it together, but somehow, she was getting by. She was hanging the children's clothes to dry across clotheslines in the courtyard one afternoon when Kotso came through the gate with a disgusted expression.

"Less than three bags of flour!" He shook his head, setting the bags down forcefully on the round table next to a basket of wet clothing. She wiped her hands on her apron and walked over to him.

"There are more soldiers in Sparta than olives on the trees! They are everywhere, and the bartering in Magoula is ridiculous. Fairness has been forgotten!" He turned to her mother Georgia, who was coming down the balcony staircase. "My apologies, dear," he offered.

"You have done your best, Kotso. No one can fault you for that," Georgia answered as she went to him with arms open.

He embraced his wife and then looked at both of them. "These hard times have a way of bringing out the worst in us Greeks." He shook his head and sat down at the table, looking slightly improved from his wife's affection.

Elaine came out of the kitchen with a glass of cold water and set it down on the table in front of him.

"Thank you, child," he said to her.

Diamanto took wet pieces of clothing out of her basket. "It's these people too," she said, verbalizing what had been on her mind for some time. "I'm sure the bartering in Vassara is fair." However grateful she felt for the new home, Diamanto couldn't warm up to the town of Magoula as she had thought she would. "They seem hardened here," she added as she returned to the clothesline and hung more pieces.

Georgia sat down next to Kotso. He took a sip from his glass and sat back, commenting, "They are. There is curtness in them that I do not find favorable. A lack of heart, you might say."

Diamanto let out a sigh. She knew the situation in Greece was getting worse. Stores had closed, and there had been increases in food rations, leading to the creation of the bartering system among locals, and with the exchange of goods becoming more difficult, there was no telling what hardships they would face to feed themselves. At first, Diamanto had been optimistic, hoping the barter system might help provide for her children, but these people were tough on each other. This wasn't the first time Kotso had left with eggs or olive oil, which he had kept in large quantity from Vassara, and returned from town disgusted with his trade. She made the best she could with what little they had but resented the unfairness.

In preparing for the main meal later that day, Diamanto pushed in Tasso's chair, keeping it in its place as if her husband would walk through the door at any moment. Cabbage soup had become a staple at the dinner table, much to the children's disliking.

George and Elaine were the last to arrive to the table while everyone waited. Her son took his seat next to Elaine and made a sour face at her when he saw the table set with bowls.

George took a whiff and asked, "Mama, why do we have to eat this disgusting soup? The smell is making me sick!"

"George, eat what is in front of you, and be grateful for it!" Kotso sternly replied.

Diamanto shot her father a look of thanks because her burden was enough to bear without difficulties from the children.

"The potatoes are almost ready," Georgia added optimistically to her grandson. "We can boil some soon."

At that moment a large German tanker headed down the main road that led into Sparta, just past the side road to their house. Everyone stopped. Diamanto's heart beat faster. The Nazis had ultimately taken over the city. She hoped Tasso had made it to base safely and had received an assignment that kept him as far from danger as possible. She exhaled deeply as the tanker went out of earshot.

Despite his grandfather's warning, George exclaimed, "Potatoes, soup, cabbage—yuck! I want meat! I want bread! I want real food!"

Diamanto couldn't hold back her sorrow. She put down her spoon and buried her face in the cloth, weeping.

"Great, George! Now look at what you've done! Isn't it enough that Baba is gone? Mama is upset enough already!" Elaine scolded.

George started to cry too and put his head on the arm of his grandfather, who was sitting next to him. Kotso patted his head.

His words muffled, George blubbered, "I'm sorry, Mama. I'm just so hungry! And I miss Baba!" George continued weeping into his grandfather's arms. Elaine started to cry too, and it didn't take long before Maria joined in. They sat and wept, all of them, until Diamanto slowly pushed her chair back and stood up at the table.

"We can't be like this." She paused to gather her composure. "It isn't right." She blotted her face with the tip of her apron and looked up at each member of the family. Georgia had calmed Maria by letting the child climb on her lap, where she was patting her back.

"Baba would be very upset to think we were falling apart like this. He asked us to be strong, remember? I'm hungry too, George." She forced a smile at her son. "We are going to have to be patient until our crops start yielding more for us to eat. Until then, we have to be stronger than this! Baba expects nothing less!" She felt her insides strengthening the more she spoke and as looked at her parents, who smiled in approval.

"Well said, Diamanto," Kotso replied.

"Yes, Mama," George sniffed. "Sorry."

"That's all right, George." She smiled as she watched Elaine wipe her cheeks with the back of her palm and sit up straighter.

Later that night, Diamanto sat on the Magoula house balcony looking at the bright stars that sparkled across the black sky, her hands resting in her lap. The children were finally at rest. Kotso came out of the upstairs door and sat next to her on an empty wooden chair. They sat in silence, and her father put his hand over hers. When he squeezed her right hand, she closed her eyes. Knowing that he approved of her efforts and that he loved her unconditionally made her feel as if she was strong enough for anything.

One morning, months later, the sound of a tank engine broke the silence of a peaceful rural morning. Diamanto went to the window without concern, having become accustomed to the sound of enemy vehicles traveling up and down the main street near her house as the Axis presence increased in Sparta. But when the entourage of jeeps turned down her dirt road, passing just below her bedroom window, she froze. The screeching sound of brakes as the vehicles came to a halt caused her to rush for the children. Moments later, she heard her mother scream from the courtyard. Diamanto rushed down the stairs with Maria in her arms and George and Elaine following closely behind. She gasped when she saw her house surrounded by over a dozen German soldiers. A Nazi officer boldly entered the gate and shouted something in German. Diamanto pulled the children close and stood near her mother, trembling.

A few soldiers passed them briskly as if they were invisible, proceeding straight through the doors into the lower level of the house. They came out just as fast as they had gone in, nodding to another German who seemed to be in charge. The same two soldiers then walked around the back of the property by the chicken coop, seemingly inspecting the area. Diamanto noticed their heavy supply of guns, along with a piercing look of hatred in their eyes. They were a horrifying sight, and for a moment, she was convinced this was the end for her family. A dozen more soldiers entered the courtyard next. Diamanto's father was nowhere in sight. She prayed he was out in the fields working or down the street at a neighbor's, out of danger.

When another officer brought a group of horses near the fields, Diamanto watched in defeat as the animals were let loose. Stomping around her beans, tomatoes, and potatoes, they sniffed and chewed the earth. The one in charge called out to a soldier sitting in a jeep parked in front of the gate. The young Nazi got out of the vehicle quickly and brought with him a man who had his hands bound behind his back. As the soldier walked him through the courtyard, Diamanto saw he was badly bruised, with a bleeding cut on his chin. George gasped aloud at the sight of the Greek prisoner, but Diamanto quickly hushed him. Georgia broke into audible tears as the bound man was led, limping, to stand in front of them. Diamanto, who did not recognize his face, held her tears back with all of her might.

The officer shook the man's arm and said something to him in German. The man nodded, and Diamanto realized his bilingual skills had been his demise. As an asset to the enemy, she assumed, the poor soul was being forced to act as an interpreter for the Nazis.

"They want your home," he muttered to her in Greek. "You have to give it to them, or they will kill all of you, including the children. Please do as they say." His voice trembled as if he had seen other atrocities with tragic outcomes.

"Our *home*?" Diamanto repeated in disbelief.

The German officer yelled something to the prisoner, and he continued. "They want it for headquarters. It is big. It's what they need," he explained.

"But where will we go?" she asked, astonished at the idea at first. Feeling her mother's touch, she turned to look at Georgia, whose expression was urgent. Elaine looked horrified.

"Let us worry about that later, dear," her mother uttered. "The children, Diamanto." The old woman put her head down after she spoke.

Suddenly, Diamanto heard her father's voice. "Your horses are ruining our fields!" he called out from the upstairs balcony. "Can't you see those are newly planted vegetables?" he continued, unaffected by their presence. Kotso raised his arm and shouted, "Tie up your horses somewhere else!"

She was shocked at her father's boldness, at the way he spoke to the Germans as if they were misbehaved children. Two Nazis went up the stairs after him. The officer in charge turned to the interpreter in the courtyard below and said something she didn't understand. The Greek prisoner answered back in German with a trembling voice and then looked up toward the balcony at Kotso.

"If I tell them what you said, they will kill you. I have explained you are upset but will obey their orders. For God's sake, old man, save your family by holding your tongue and do as they say!" He turned and looked at Diamanto again with concern.

She knew her father's tone had needed no translation. His anger was obvious. The soldiers reached Kotso on the balcony and grabbed him, leading him toward the edge of the stone staircase as he tried to kick himself loose. Diamanto screamed, fearing the Nazis would throw him over the railing or shoot him. There was a loud crack and a painful cry for help.

"Stop!" she shouted.

"No!" yelled Georgia as the children began to scream as well. The German soldiers had him by each arm and were leading him toward the edge of the balcony's stone staircase.

"Not this house!" he continued to protest as they brought him closer to the top stair.

"Grandfather!" George and Elaine yelled as Diamanto pulled the children's faces into her skirt, shielding their eyes from the ugly scene. In one forceful push, the soldiers threw the old man down the stairs. Diamanto watched in horror as he struggled to brace himself. His delicate body tumbled down the stairs, hitting every concrete step until he reached the bottom. She ran to Kotso, throwing her body over his to shield him from the two soldiers who followed, drawing their guns over his body.

"Don't shoot! Please don't kill him!" She lifted her head to the interpreter. "Tell them they can have the house! They can have it all!" She lifted her father's face into her hands, assessing his state, grateful to see he was still conscious and breathing. When the prisoner translated, the German officer yelled out, and the other Nazis put their guns away. She gently helped her father sit up and held him in her arms. "Father, Father," she cried.

The German officer began to address her in short sentences she didn't comprehend. The interpreter spoke right after in Greek.

"We take the house. We take what's inside. We are not here to kill, but we will if provoked. Any resistance will end in death." The German officer's tone was quick, stern, and emotionless. She watched the German look straight ahead as he spoke, not making eye contact with her or anyone else. As if he was repeating a speech from memory recited many times before, he appeared disconnected from the atrocities of his army. When the Greek prisoner finished translating, the German officer held up a finger to indicate he had one more instruction.

He continued through the interpreter. "You may come to your fields during the day. You may work your crops. We will see to it that you take only enough to feed yourselves. The rest, we keep. By sundown you must obey the curfew, or you will be shot. That is all." With that, he snapped on his heels and turned, walking back toward the jeep.

Another soldier came forward and said, "You may gather your things quickly. Essentials only. Then leave the premises at once."

Diamanto's mother approached her with the children. They sat around her father, hugging him, asking him if he was all right. His left cheek was cut, but remarkably, no bones seemed broken. While her mother tended to him, Diamanto hastily went to the second floor and made a skirmish through the bedrooms, gathering clothing for her parents and children. What few photos of Tasso and her parents lay around on side tables, she slipped in between the clothing, suspecting the Germans might destroy anything left behind. She quickly pulled a handmade cloth from the side table by her bed. A glass of water fell to the floor. She left the mess. More treasured to her was this sentimental item from her mother's dowry, a cloth doily her grandmother had crocheted for Georgia's wedding. She knew her mother would be grateful.

Stopping at the family's shelf of icons, she looked up at the collection that hung over her head and grabbed a hand-painted icon depicting Jesus, Virgin Mary, and St. Basil. There was no monetary value in the icon because it was made of wood. But Diamanto sought to salvage the icon because it was priceless in her eyes; her father's grandfather had given it to Kotso when he was a young boy. Putting the religious heirloom in her bag, she paused for a moment and caught her breath.

Looking up at the icon of the Virgin Mary holding baby Jesus, she focused on the image of mother and child. *This is your duty*, she heard in her head. Diamanto looked at the icon, feeling the Mother of God staring back at her, sharing strength and love. A sense of warmth ran over her body, and she made the sign of the cross in obedience to a reaffirmed purpose. Her responsibilities centered solely on the children, and God would give her the perseverance to accomplish this task. Dwelling on hardship would serve no purpose. With deepening faith, she would prevail in protecting them.

Feeling the pressure of time, Diamanto shoved pants, shirts, and dresses into a pillowcase and took the blanket off of her bed. She walked over to the wardrobe with a tear running down her cheek. She gently kissed the door as she closed it softly, bidding farewell to the beloved gift from her husband.

Descending the stairs with her items, she let out a sigh of relief when she saw her father sitting up in a chair at the base of the stairs, sipping a glass of water. He held a kerchief to his face. She stayed at her father's side along with the children and her mother, tying up her pillowcases, while German soldiers carried away her dishes and serveware. She looked up to see bedding taken out of the courtyard and thrown into a pile in the back of one jeep, while others things, such as glasses and silverware, were loaded into the vehicles behind it.

As contents were taken away, strangely marked cardboard packages with Nazi swastikas were brought into the courtyard, carried right past them, and lined up against the terrace railing. One soldier struggled as he brought in a metal box, the likes of which she had never seen before. It looked like some sort of machine. A long roll extended across the top. She watched as her children stared at the strange contraption too.

Shortly thereafter, she and her parents, along with the children, were shuffled out of the front gate. They stood together on the outside looking in, as their home went under immediate transformation. Elaine looked terrified, while George looked up at his mother with confusion in his eyes. Diamanto stroked his hair and told him that she would explain things later and that she was proud of their obedience, reiterating that their grandfather was going to be well. This was all that mattered, she told them, feeling grateful her husband wasn't present to witness such injustice.

As they stood, she heard Georgia whisper to her father, "I don't understand, Kotso. Why this house? What do they want with it?"

"It's exactly what they want," he said to her. "It's new, it's off the main road, and it's large. With their animals and their supplies, this is what they want for storage. From the looks of it, they're going to work out of the upstairs." He paused. "Tasso and I talked about this risk, but we hoped because it was set back a bit from the road, perhaps the Germans would miss it."

Diamanto looked at her father, puzzled. "He never said anything to me."

"He didn't want to alarm you," he replied. "Really, Diamanto, we are lucky those devils are letting us keep anything from our fields, even though everything will be destroyed if those animals don't stop trampling our crops!" The old man started to speak too loud. Diamanto hushed her father, still trembling from fear.

"We should have stayed in Vassara," Georgia said, shaking her head.

"No, my dear," answered Kotso. "That would have put Tasso in grave danger. We could not take that risk."

Diamanto had no time to contemplate the past. Although she was glad to have saved a few items, none of the material possessions mattered to her as she looked at the faces of her children.

As a group of Nazi soldiers stood behind by the last jeep in line, one of them yelled at Elaine's mama. She wanted to shout right back at him for all that they had done to her grandfather, but she knew better. Hadn't Mama been through enough? What more could these animals want? He motioned for them to stand back and said something she didn't understand. The interpreter had driven off in another vehicle, but she didn't need him to explain the Germans wanted her family out of the way. Her mama motioned for her to move with George, and they did. George was staring at the soldiers intently, and that really bothered her. She nudged him and told him to stop it, but her little brother kept staring. Elaine had had enough, and when she caught him looking at the soldiers again while her grandparents were busy talking to Mama, she shoved him.

"I said stop it!" she scolded.

One of the Germans soldiers saw this and let out a small laugh, which bothered her even more. When he removed his army cap, she caught a glimpse of his thin, blonde, straight hair brushed to the side. He replaced the cap on his head and then reached into his satchel and pulled out a small bundle of material. His skin was pale like the rest of them, and she didn't like his green eyes. He unwrapped the cloth he was holding and offered a piece of something to her brother.

"What is that?" George asked her.

"I don't know … It might be cheese," she said, not trusting the stranger.

"Why does it have holes?" George pressed on.

She turned to face her brother and exhaled loudly. Why couldn't he just stand there and be quiet like her? "I don't know," she snapped. "Don't take it, or Mama will be very angry!" Exhausted by her brother's ignorance, she let out another sigh. They had bigger problems. Where would they go? Would they return to the village? What would happen to their home? Would they be taken prisoner? She had once overheard a neighbor talking about horrific places where people were sent, far away.

"But I'm hungry! If it's cheese, I want some!" George persisted.

She repeated her warning but suddenly realized she had taken her eyes off of Maria. Panic set in for a second before she heard the girl's voice say, "Thank you."

Elaine froze as she watched her little sister take a thick slice from the German soldier's hand and put it in her mouth. Maria's face lit up with a giant smile as she chewed, and the green-eyed soldier chuckled more.

Reaching for Maria, Elaine looked at George with wide eyes. Whatever she was eating, Maria seemed to like it. She looked at their mama, who thankfully hadn't seen what had just happened. Then the soldier pulled another thick piece from his cloth bundle and held it out. George feverishly reached forward and grabbed it, quickly putting the slice into his mouth before Elaine could object. She gasped as both of her siblings stood together, chomping. She peered at them indignantly. If Mama had seen any of this, she would be scolded for sure.

The soldier kept laughing, which only increased her contempt, and when he removed a third piece, he offered it directly to her. His fake smile didn't fool her. Elaine squinted her eyes and shook her head, turning away.

But he bent down and held it out again, saying quietly in broken Greek, "For you."

She felt only angry at first, but then she thought about her empty stomach. From the smiles on George and Maria's faces, it seemed to taste good. George nodded to her as if to say, *Take it, stupid! It's delicious!* She was famished and couldn't remember the last time she had eaten something with flavor. Elaine looked at Mama again, who was still distracted. She glanced back again at George. His expression was urgent. She decided to take it. But just as Elaine placed the slice in her mouth, her mother shouted, "Children!" Her voice seemed stern.

Elaine froze and swallowed hard to get rid of the evidence in her mouth. She took a step to the left to hide George, who was chewing as if he were at a family feast.

Before Elaine could utter a word in her defense, there was a loud noise from upstairs. A soldier standing on the balcony called down to the soldier who had offered them the food. He immediately rewrapped the item in his cloth, placed the bundle in the back of the jeep, and then ran up the stairs. Elaine brought George and Maria over to their mama as they all looked up to see what was happening. Several men were inside the upstairs bedroom, from where the repeated banging emanated. The sound grew louder and louder, and the Germans kept shouting. Elaine watched her mama walk over to the iron gates to get a better view of the upstairs balcony. Elaine joined her mama and gasped when she saw them attempting to push the wardrobe out of the house.

Her grandfather lifted his head wearily from where he sat and said with a smirk, "Elaine, don't fret. Your baba added the legs and top part to that chest *inside* the bedroom, remember? There's no way they'll get it through the door!" His injured face displayed a satisfied grin.

"What if they destroy it out of anger?" her mama asked him.

The old man shook his head. The banging continued for a few more minutes and then suddenly stopped. Through the open doorway to the upstairs, Elaine watched with relief as the German soldiers placed the wardrobe back in its original place. It appeared they had given up and were going to leave Mama's gift where it was.

Chapter Thirteen

"Why are so many Germans here?" asked Georgia one evening as the family headed to their rented room in Sparta. It was nothing more than an empty bedroom inside the home of one of Kotso's cousins, an elderly man and his wife who had lost their son early in the war. Diamanto was relieved they had somewhere to stay. Kotso and Georgia slept in the couple's sitting room, and she and the children had been given a small room with one bed. There was little money to offer in return for the roof over their heads, but Kotso arranged to bring them food from Magoula each day out of what they could take from their fields. Diamanto's high opinion of her father's abilities never ceased; the old man's reputation was one of honesty and integrity. She had met the couple only once before as a young girl and could tell the loss of their son devastated them. They were warm and welcoming, and she appreciated their hospitality.

Streets bustled during that time of day in downtown Sparta as everyone rushed home before curfew. Mothers hurried their children along, calling their names anxiously, to gather behind closed doors as night fell. There had been a drastic change in the city from only a few months earlier. Young men were gone, secured behind their own defenses.

"The Germans occupy our city now, my dear," explained Kotso to his wife as they continued walking at a brisk pace. Diamanto heard her father explain the situation with gentleness. He was a patient man, she thought, and she was grateful he never tired of her mother's unending questions. But she sympathized with Georgia, who up until then had led a simple life in the village, rarely leaving Vassara.

"Why are those soldiers stretching that wire across the street?" inquired George. "We didn't see *that* this morning!"

"I have no idea, son," she replied.

Looking farther ahead, she saw a group of German soldiers unrolling a large bale of barbed wire with their hands, protected by heavy gloves. They proceeded down the street with the wire, stretching it to run parallel with the sidewalks. When the soldiers reached the end of the street, they cut the wire with strange-looking hand tools. She stopped to take in the horrible scene of the familiar city becoming almost unrecognizable. The rest of the family stood watching as well. Sparta was distorted into a maze of wire tangled across shops and businesses, down streets they had once walked freely.

"Well, if the wire is there, we won't be able to go across!" said Elaine.

"That's exactly their purpose," explained Kotso. "This must be their way of controlling who comes in and out of the city."

Diamanto felt her heart beat fast. Letting out a deep sigh, she said, "That's ridiculous. They have us caged in like animals." She put her head down, disgusted with the ugly changes. They were being treated more like wild beasts than like people.

Biting her lip to keep it together, she touched the small gold cross around her neck, praying for strength while the accumulation of anxiety pushed her mental limits. Worrying about Tasso and his safety was bad enough. She hadn't received any word. She constantly wondered whether he had made it safely to his unit before the Germans came. Where was he? Had he been taken prisoner? Would she see him again? What would happen to their home? How long could they spend their days caring for the crops, only to have the Germans take most of the yield? The sleepless nights left her without energy, and her emotional strength was waning. There was an unending stream of negative thoughts in the back of her mind that she worked hard to ignore.

The next day, Diamanto spent the better part of the morning trying to harvest what tomatoes remained in her field, picking the imperfect ones, bruised and somewhat crushed, off the ground, not wanting to waste any. Kotso and Georgia picked beans nearby. Diamanto stopped for a moment and sat on the ground to rest, looking around her field, toward the house where the Nazis were walking through her bedrooms, sitting in her courtyard, washing with her water.

A breeze blew overhead, ruffling the silvery leaves on nearby olive trees. Gazing up at the landscape with Mount Taygetos in the background, she noticed that the blue sky was interrupted by a cluster of graying clouds. Perhaps rain was coming, she predicted from the transforming wind.

With the breeze, a soft scent of orange mixed with floral tones blew across the field from citrus trees down the road on the opposite property. The valley bore little resemblance to high-altitude villages, such as Vassara. As she inhaled the sweet-smelling air, she smiled for a moment, reminding herself that all living things flourished with ease in Magoula. Holding a handful of tomatoes in her palm, she inspected their size, amazed at the area's rich soil. *A farmer's dream*, she thought, imagining the bountiful harvest that would have been if the Nazis hadn't come. Her smile vanished as she softly whispered, "This was supposed to be our paradise." She turned a tomato over, noticing its blemish. "And now the serpent has poisoned my Eden, bringing evil and death."

She looked up, concerned, when she heard her mother's groan. Georgia wasn't one to complain easily. "What is it, Mother?" she asked Georgia, who had hunched over and appeared out of breath. Kotso went to his wife's side and tried to help her straighten.

"It's my back," she said. "I felt something pull, and now I can't stand. It will pass." The old woman gave Diamanto a smile the daughter knew to be false, one Georgia forced whenever she was in pain. Diamanto wasn't fooled by her mother's attempt to downplay her obvious suffering.

"She just needs to sit awhile," called Kotso. Diamanto's father was no better at the art of deception and often partnered with his wife to keep others from fussing.

From a nearby field, the children came running. Elaine carried little Maria, who was hysterical.

"What's wrong?" she asked Elaine.

"It's her doll. She's been asking for it all morning," Elaine explained. "Says she can't find the doll anywhere in our things, and I know it's not back in Sparta."

As Maria wailed loudly, Diamanto grew concerned about the volume.

She didn't want them to call attention to themselves in the field since they had been warned to work quietly.

"Maria, calm down!" Diamanto insisted.

The child didn't listen, and as the screaming continued, George tried to talk over his sister's tantrum. "I don't think we ever brought her doll out from the house, Mama." He pointed over to the courtyard, to their home filled with Germans. "Her doll is probably still in *there*!"

"I waaaaant my doll!" Maria screamed.

"Oh, children, if her doll is in there, it's gone. There's no way of getting it now." She tried to console Maria while watching Kotso help her mother uneasily lower her body onto a spread-out blanket, with Georgia clenching his arm.

"Please, children, please!" Diamanto sat down too, right in the dirt of the tomato patch, and rocked Maria as the little girl's cries slowly lessened to an ongoing moan.

Diamanto closed her eyes, holding Maria's head tightly to her chest and rocking her, humming a quiet hymn of the church. Wiping the little one's tears, she held back her own. Like Georgia, she too wanted to hide her pain from her children. After a while Maria started to fall asleep in Diamanto's arms. She let her daughter rest as Elaine and George sat with their grandfather under the tree, holding Georgia's hands and trying to comfort their grandmother.

Later that afternoon, while the heat continued, and with only a few hours left on their property, Diamanto asked Kotso if she could leave the children in his care for a moment. Georgia appeared to be feeling better, so she left Maria resting on a blanket while Kotso and the older two children searched for any potatoes in the ground that the Germans might have missed.

Diamanto walked closer to her house with care. Knowing a German soldier stood armed in the courtyard at all times, she worried he might mistake her for someone else and shoot, but determination overtook her fear. Avoiding eye contact, she kept her head down and proceeded carefully to the chicken coop. They were allowed to remove only three eggs each day, as if that could sustain her family. Diamanto didn't dare sneak more. Typically, she had George along for the task because the boy enjoyed searching the nests for eggs as if it were a game. But on this day, she had come alone. Risky, she knew, to be a woman near enemy soldiers, but she needed to be alone, even if only for a few minutes.

Stepping into the low-ceilinged coop, she looked around the dark room while noisy chickens clucked around her. She winced at the smell as she looked down at hay scattered across the floor and picked up the long straw basket she kept near the doorway. Observing the chickens, she was almost jealous of their ignorance, oblivious to the atrocities existing outside their environment. After placing three eggs into the basket, she stood in the middle of the room and gently set the basket on the floor at her feet.

Wringing her hands, she felt heaviness build in her chest. Instinctively, she quietly called out her husband's name. "Tasso? Taaaaassoooooo!" She knew he couldn't hear her, but on some level, she believed he did and repeated his name over and over. She fell to her knees and put her head in her hands, weeping with desperation, as if she could wish him back into her arms.

"I need you, Tasso. I need you so badly! What am I to do? The children, Tasso! They need you!" She thought of her mother, worried for her parents' well-being, and cried more. Tears turned to moans. On her knees, she looked up to the ceiling and made the sign of the cross.

"Please, Mother of God, heal my mother. Comfort my family through the horrors this war brings. Please, Panayia, keep my family strong. Keep the children safe. Let no evil beset them." She paused and looked down at her lap. "And please, God, grant me strength as well. Help me to hold it together until Tasso returns." When she said his name aloud again, her heartache set in further. "And above all, please return my Tassouli to me. Protect him so he can come back to us again."

She sat for a while with her eyes closed, in a moment of peace. After a few minutes, she opened her eyes, picked up her basket of eggs, and stood erect. With a calm voice, she said softly, "I'll do the best I can, Tasso. For your sake." Sunlight streamed into the darkened coop, and Diamanto turned quickly, fearing she heard a Nazi. As the door to the coop opened and fresh air came in, she saw that it was George who stood in the doorway, holding Maria's hand.

"Grandfather fell asleep," he said with a look of hesitation on his face. Maria let go of her brother and held out a purple wildflower.

"For you, Mama," the little girl said with a smile, although the redness from many hours of meltdown hadn't left her face. Diamanto smiled back, opening her arms wide to her children. They came into her arms, and she held them tight.

"For you, dear Lord," she said aloud, feeling the love of her children as well as the love of Tasso, who she imagined was reaching out the only way he could.

Weeks blended into months as time seemed lost in a similar pattern of hardship. They maintained work in the fields by day and returned to Sparta before curfew. Their walk back to the city was always difficult. The children never wanted to leave Magoula. Her parents were often tired and sore, and everyone was hungry. Diamanto felt strain in her legs as well, but without a carriage, they had to go home by foot.

"Can we stop and rest for a while? I'm exhausted!" Elaine asked on the way to Sparta one afternoon.

"I want to stop too. Mama, my feet hurt!" George added.

"We have to keep going, children. Curfew will be here soon, and we have to be inside. We're almost there." Diamanto carried Maria, who had fallen asleep. Her back ached as she held the heavy toddler. Both children moaned at her answer.

Sparta grew ominous. Families started selling household items on the streets to get money for food. The peddlers were aggressive, with desperation in their eyes. She feared one day they might grab her satchels, and she carried them in a guarded manner.

News in the papers reported the rise of resistance groups forming across Greece, which in turn seemed to make the German soldiers less tolerant of Greek people. There were beatings and raids on homes belonging to those suspected of hoarding food. Graffiti appeared on government buildings, and there were rumors of the youth trying to organize themselves against the government. The city, like the entire country, was in a state of increased unrest.

As long barbed-wire fencing stretched across streets, heavier layers of wire blocked Sparta's main street, nearly halting traffic and keeping anything from moving without detection. Only small openings at corners allowed passage for pedestrians, while preventing carriages or animals from passing through. Burnt buildings left shelled-out recollections of homes Diamanto had once known. Greeks kept their heads down as they walked and barely greeted one another. The tension was palpable.

With schools now closed by the Germans, Diamanto had the added task of keeping Elaine and George busy and maintaining their math and reading skills. She was disappointed for many reasons, including the fact that Elaine and George seemed to enjoy the larger schools of Sparta. Kotso kept a small Bible in his breast pocket at all times and used it to provide the children a lesson whenever possible. He had them read passages and questioned their comprehension. She loved how he tended to the children, keeping an eye on their play and teaching them Greek history through his colorful stories of ancient times and the liberation of their country from the Turks.

As time progressed, Diamanto witnessed her home changing a little more each day. The house looked colder in the morning light, void of the warmth she and Tasso had once created. Pots of flowers in the courtyard were either missing or left dead, unattended. Occasionally, the door to the upstairs foyer was propped open, giving her the chance to see what was going on inside. They wanted fresh air, she guessed. Diamanto took those opportunities to catch a glimpse of the bedrooms for as far as she could see while standing at the gate below. Ever fearful of being caught, she looked quickly, noticing maps of Greece with red markings and black Xs nailed to the walls of the front foyer. Amazed at how the home had morphed into a cold, stark, office-like dwelling so quickly, she thought the structure looked more like a business than a house. She and her parents also watched the lower level transform into a storage facility for the Nazis' equipment, the walls stacked high with boxes of unidentified items, crates marked with the Nazi symbol.

In contrast, the fields remained free, providing peaceful familiarity to the children, a memory of a preoccupation life. The orchard's land, although still void of lemon and orange trees, remained cleared, awaiting Tasso's homecoming. She was thankful the children had an oasis. The fields appeared to be the only place that remained somewhat similar.

One morning, as the family arrived in Magoula just after sunrise for a long day of watering, weeding, gathering, and cleaning, Elaine shouted out in excitement.

"Look!" the girl exclaimed as they approached their tomato patch.

"Elaine, quiet down," her grandmother warned.

Diamanto peered nervously through the trees and saw a group of Nazis sitting in the courtyard, having breakfast at her table. One of the soldiers stood up and turned to face them in the fields, putting both hands on his hips. She was certain he was watching them.

"Elaine! They heard you! You must keep quiet!" she warned with a stern expression.

"But Mama, look!" Elaine said to her, running to a tall tomato plant and pointing to the ground next to a branch of green tomatoes. Diamanto could see there was something lying on the ground.

"What is that?" she asked her daughter.

Elaine held up a ragged doll. "It's Maria's doll!"

Maria let out a scream and ran to her sister, grabbing the doll and clutching it to her chest.

Elaine bent down to pick up something else. "And my brush! My brush from America that Aunt Pota sent me! Remember?" she asked excitedly.

Diamanto didn't know what to think. How could these long-lost items appear out of nowhere?

"And that's my ball!" said George, picking up a small blue ball from the ground near the bean plants.

"Children! Where on Earth did you find those things?"

"Mama! They were right here," Elaine said, pointing, "next to the plants!"

Diamanto looked at Kotso. He seemed equally suspicious with his raised eyebrow.

Before Diamanto could instruct her daughter, Kotso said gently, "Elaine and George … listen to me. Take your things and put them in our bag under the tree. I'm not sure what is happening, but you must remember that we are always being watched." He pointed with his eyes toward the courtyard. "We don't know their intentions, so be quiet and do your work diligently. We don't want trouble."

Diamanto nodded.

"Yes, Grandfather," they said in unison, putting their things away with smiles on their faces.

Diamanto told Maria that she could keep her doll as long as she was quiet like the others. The little girl smiled and hugged the toy tightly while her mother breathed a sigh of relief. Perhaps this meant an easier time for the day's chores.

As they continued their work, Diamanto pondered the sudden appearance of the items. She looked over again at the Germans sitting in her courtyard. Four of them were busy at the table, looking down at papers, but a fifth soldier stood watching her family at the fence. A cold chill came over her body as she wondered what he wanted. She was about to look away but realized in that moment he was the same Nazi who had given the children food the day the Germans took her home. He held one of her cups and saucers in his hand, and as he raised the cup to take a sip, he held it out to her, smiling. She put her head down at once, afraid to make eye contact with the enemy. *Did he do this?* Diamanto wondered, turning away to resume pruning. She was too terrified to speculate about his motives.

When they left for Sparta later that day, the children were noticeably upbeat. No one complained while walking to town, no one asked if they could stop to rest, and most surprisingly, none of them said they were hungry. Despite the long day's work, there was almost a skip in their steps. She was glad something had made them happy.

Once they reached the city, George ran a little too far ahead to chase his ball. He refused to hold Georgia's hand, which he always did when they walked the main street, passing through the center of town. They continued down the barbed-wired area, and Diamanto called after him once more, telling him to slow down and hang on to his ball. They were just about to pass the main drag of Sparta, where a long line of mature palm trees stood in a row, lining the center median.

As if a last testament to the city's eternal beauty and Spartan strength, reminiscent of the ancient warriors at Thermopolis, the palms stood perfectly erect and tall, seeming to resist arrest in their own right, refusing submission to the oppressor. Burnt-out houses and crushed buildings ripped apart the city, Diamanto thought, but the giant palm trees remained strong in defiance. She wondered whether she was the only person to notice the trees, hoping instead that their perseverance gave others hope, even if only in secret.

George disobeyed yet again and skipped ahead, chasing after his ball that had rolled away.

"George, I've said it before. Stop and wait for the rest of us!" Diamanto called out.

"I can't lose my ball again!" George yelled back indignantly, running ahead.

"George!" his older sister yelled as she let go of her grandfather's hand and started out after him.

"No, Elaine! Stop!" cried Diamanto.

Elaine turned to answer her mama. "I'm going to catch him."

George picked up the pace to outrun his sister and tripped, falling headfirst into the barbed wire fence.

"*George*!" cried Diamanto. She rushed to the boy's side as he lay adjacent to the fence, his face badly cut by the wire. Blood streamed down George's cheek from his left eye socket. Kotso fell to the boy's body while Georgia grabbed Maria in her arms.

"I can't see! I can't see!" he wailed.

"No, not my George! Not my George!" Diamanto collapsed on the ground, enveloping her son.

Kotso got up and ran to a pair of Nazi soldiers standing at the next corner. Diamanto could hear her father pleading with them in Greek to follow. She looked up and called after Kotso that they wouldn't understand what he was trying to say. She feared he would be shot for bothering them, but one of the soldiers went with him and headed her way. She could hardly breathe as she watched her son in agony. She felt helpless and trembled while holding his bleeding head. The German soldier bent down and looked at her. He pointed to himself and nodded at her, speaking some words she didn't comprehend. But then he took his hand and placed it on top of hers and said in Greek, "Doctor."

She exhaled and nodded to him in return, still unsure of what was happening. But she knew her son could bleed to death if they didn't get him help soon. She was desperate. In a flash, the Nazi scooped up George and quickly proceeded down the street, carrying him in his arms. She hurried to go with him. Kotso followed. Georgia came along too, still carrying Maria and holding Elaine's hand.

The soldier turned, motioning for them to hurry. After two blocks, they reached Sparta's medical facility, now under Nazi control.

George was quickly carried inside the building, past the armed guards, and behind a white curtain. A blonde German woman wearing a white uniform stood next to an armed guard and held out her hand to stop Diamanto. She pointed for her to sit in a chair, and Diamanto gasped, but her father told her to obey, assuring her that he would stay at George's side. Another soldier came from behind the curtain where George had been taken and said something to the uniformed lady, pointing at Kotso. The German woman stepped aside as Kotso was led past the curtain.

Diamanto couldn't feel her body as she waited. If anything horrible happened to her son, she'd never forgive herself. A German soldier brought another chair for Georgia, and Elaine stood next to them while little Maria climbed atop her grandmother's lap. Diamanto looked at her mother and daughter, unable to talk. Her eyes wandered around the white, clean room that smelled of chemicals. She felt like she had entered another world because the medical facility was cleaner than any Greek hospital she had ever seen. There was strange-looking equipment on one side of the room, next to large machines. German nurses rushed around in stiff, starched uniforms, wearing Nazi markings on their white coats.

Diamanto listened closely to hear her son from behind the curtain. All she could see of her father was his feet, recognizable by his tattered shoes, different from the shiny footwear of the doctor and soldier. They spoke in low tones in their foreign language. Her son's cries struck her heart to the point where she almost fainted. Elaine cried too, so Diamanto held on to her daughter's hand tightly. *They have been through so much*, she thought. *How much more can these children take?*

Just then, Georgia reached over and gripped Diamanto and Elaine's joined hands, squeezing tightly as the women listened to moans coming from behind the white curtain. Georgia wept into her youngest grandchild's blanket as she held little Maria in her lap.

Almost two hours later, Kotso emerged with a look of exhausted relief. He explained that he had watched as George's gash across his eyelid was sewn with several stitches.

"I wish we could communicate with them," he said, "but I know they saved his eye."

"Does George have to stay here?" Elaine inquired.

"No," Kotso answered.

"What do we do now?" Diamanto asked her father.

"We take him home," Kotso answered.

A nurse came from behind the curtain and handed him a small glass bottle with a clear liquid inside of it, along with a package of bandages. She rambled on in German. Kotso shook his head.

"What's she saying?" Elaine asked.

"I don't know," Diamanto said, exhausted from the ordeal.

The nurse looked at Elaine and then at Diamanto. "Keep clean," she said in broken Greek.

"Yes," Kotso said with relief. "Thank you."

Diamanto stood up. "Thank you," she said to the German nurse.

The woman just looked at her with a blank stare and then turned on her heels and left the room while Diamanto made the sign of the cross and took a deep breath. She smiled at her mother, feeling for the first and last time a moment of gratitude to the Germans.

Chapter Fourteen

Nighttime hours became increasingly ominous. Despite feeling exhausted from the long hours of work, Diamanto battled with insomnia at the end of each day. With bombs exploding in the distance, she found it impossible to sleep in the rented room. One night, she was awoken by a loud crack that shook the house. Even Kotso woke up and appeared by her bedside.

"Are you all right?" he asked.

"That was another bomb, wasn't it?" she asked, sitting up. She looked over at the children, who slept peacefully.

"Not sure. It felt closer than before." He rubbed his head and went over to the window.

She watched her father's shadow as he peered out into the night. She felt sorry for him in his aged state, separated from his villagers and the life he had always known. She wished his days could be peacefully lazy, with nothing to do but sit in Vassara's square, play cards, drink coffee, and debate the weather with childhood friends. *That's what the seniors years are meant for*, she thought. His face appeared overcome with concern as he looked out onto the occupied city. They didn't belong here. They should be home.

"You must miss Vassara as much as I do," she said.

He sighed. "More than you know … But it doesn't do any good for us to think of that now. We *had* to leave. Tasso had to get with his unit. It's good that he worked on the house, even if the Germans are in it tonight." After a moment, he added, "Someday, it will be yours again."

Diamanto fought back tears as she thought of her lovely home and all the effort her husband had put into finishing it. Once again the dark night became quiet, and Kotso shuffled over to her bed and kissed her on her forehead as if she were a little girl.

"I'm proud of you, Diamanto," he said. Tears instantly welled up in her eyes again. "You are holding it together well. The children are strong because of *you*, and in that way, you honor your husband."

She felt his hand on her cheek and held it there with both her hands. She wanted to be little again, free from responsibility, away from danger. Wishing she could blink her eyes and be back in Vassara as a young girl, she cupped her father's fingers against her wet cheek. Kotso stayed close and placed his other hand on her back, soothing her pain. She looked across the room at George, sleeping soundly with his bandaged eye. She had to think of the here and now.

"I love you, Father," she said.

"I love you too, my child. Get some rest," he answered.

She lay back down, closing her eyes even though she wouldn't be able to sleep.

The next morning, as the family left their room in Sparta, Elaine pointed at something. "Didn't notice those before!" she exclaimed.

"What, my girl?" Diamanto asked.

"Those trees. Look! They are full of fruit on top!" Elaine said, pointing again.

"Can we pick some, Mama?" asked George.

Maria grew excited, just what Diamanto wanted to avoid. "Oranges! Oranges!" the little one cried out.

"Absolutely not! They don't belong to us, children!" She looked at them sincerely.

"But if no one is eating them …" George protested.

"No, George!" she repeated. "We are *guests* here. Don't forget that."

"Listen to Mama!" Kotso added.

"Awwww. I'll bet no one would notice," the boy said, sulking.

Elaine persisted too. "A few oranges wouldn't …"

"Elaine," Kotso said sternly, "Mama said no."

Diamanto exhaled, grateful her father had ended the back and forth.

The rest of their walk to Magoula was quiet, until they neared their house from the main road. Diamanto could hear shouting coming from their home. She looked at her father with concern. Germans were yelling at one another, seeming to be in an intense argument. Doors slammed. Loud voices called out foreign words she didn't understand, but it was clear the men were angry. Elaine and George looked at her with fear. Slowing their pace as they approached, Georgia and Kotso grabbed the hands of George and Elaine while Diamanto picked up Maria in her arms. When they got to the gate, Diamanto looked upstairs toward the balcony and saw a German throwing his hands up in the air before walking back inside. Another door slammed from inside. She wished she knew what they were saying.

"There's definitely trouble," her father said softly. "I wonder if it has to do with what I heard in town yesterday. Even the papers wrote about them losing their hold against Allied forces. Perhaps it's true. Maybe this war's end is in sight."

"Let it be so," Georgia said softly.

Kotso turned to George and Elaine. "Let's make sure we work quietly today. No running. No screaming," he advised.

"Yes, Grandfather," they replied.

Diamanto put Maria down but held her hand tightly as they walked, hoping the fighting wouldn't escalate. They worked a long, hard day in the fields. The sun was particularly hot, and the children were sluggish walking home. She looked up the street as they neared the perimeter of the city and noticed the same distraught look on Greek faces everywhere. New graffiti appeared on what once had been public municipal buildings, currently overrun by the Germans. One of the handwritten slogans boldly read, "Eirini," the Greek word for "peace," in all capital letters.

Along the residential streets stretched a line of people selling their possessions, like a strange bazaar. The sellers bore an expression of desperation on their faces. There were women who didn't look up from the street but held out items, asking if anyone wanted to buy them. They wore tattered clothing and grim expressions, and their thin, frail bodies were a drastic sight. *They are slowly starving to death*, Diamanto surmised with sadness. She looked at her mother's devastated expression, knowing the sight of these poor families broke Georgia's heart as well.

There were old men, women, and children selling bed frames, pieces of silver, and jewelry. But no one had money to buy anything. Small children sat on the curb with their mothers, holding outstretched hands in desperation. As she walked past them, they looked up with pathetic stares. None of their things held importance in this time of hunger, she thought. All they wanted was money for food. She gripped tightly the bag of vegetables she carried to barter for their rented room and feed themselves.

That night, the children seemed impossible. Even after they ate, George and Elaine both asked for more and accused each other of eating more than their share. Her children's growing bodies required heartier food, she knew, but all they had was what they grew.

"I'm still hungry, Mama," Elaine complained.

"I'm still hungry too. Can we have something else?" asked George.

It didn't take long for their baby sister to chime in. "Me too, Mama!" Maria said.

She did her best to comfort the children. She covered their slim bodies with hard, coarse blankets, spreading them across their legs to enclose their limbs. She tucked George and Maria in like a cocoon.

Elaine proceeded to complain, "I can't sleep when I'm this hungry!"

Diamanto offered one last response. "I'm sorry. There is nothing to eat right now. Fall asleep, and when we wake up, we will eat, I promise." She was sad for her children and frustrated she couldn't offer more. Elaine's face grew despondent.

"Children! Go to sleep! You know better than to burden your mama!" Kotso chided as he stood above them, looking down at Elaine.

Unlike other nights, when she was restless, Diamanto was exhausted from the day. She sat on the bed and closed her eyes to experience the only private, personal moment she could. Ever fearful of the night, she focused her mind on Tasso, hoping he was resting comfortably somewhere safe and thinking of her. Trying to capture a brief moment of cherished solace, she planned to get up and wash her face after the children fell completely asleep, but without realizing it, she too fell into a deep slumber.

She awoke a short time later to another explosion. Sitting up quickly, Diamanto looked around the room's blackness and struggled to turn up the light on the oil lamp next to the bed. Maria was asleep, but the older two children were gone. Springing up from the bed, she tripped on a bundled-up blanket. Diamanto tumbled onto her father's legs, waking him as she braced her fall.

"What is it?" Kotso asked groggily.

"The kids, they're not here!" She hastily put shoes on her bare feet and headed for the door.

"Diamanto, wait!" he called after her.

"Where are they?" she asked, looking down the short hallway. Her heart beat hard and fast in her chest. She felt her hands turn cold. They were not in the kitchen. *Where could they be?* she wondered. She was proceeding toward the front door to the house when suddenly the entire house shook as a bomb went off close by. She heard muffled cries.

"George! Elaine!" Her voice trembled as her father came running behind her.

"Where could they have gone?" he asked.

"I don't know!" she said in a panic, running back into the kitchen.

Georgia came running into the room, holding Maria in her arms. The little girl rubbed her eyes and buried her head in Georgia's neck. The landlord couple came to the kitchen as well.

"It's the children," Georgia said, turning to them. "We can't find the older ones."

Diamanto tried to listen as she continued to hear the soft sounds of whimpering. Kotso ran to the window and opened the shutter.

"My Lord!" he exclaimed. Kotso ran to the door, and Diamanto followed him with no concern for safety. If soldiers were out there, she didn't care. All she was focused on was the children. When they exited the door, she saw her son standing next to the orange trees in back of the property. George ran into Kotso's arms as soon as he saw his grandfather.

"I'm sorry! I'm sorry! We thought we would die!" The boy clutched Kotso's waist and buried his head in the old man's torso. As Kotso hurried George back into the house, handing him over to his grandmother, Elaine cried out. She was high up in the branches of one of the orange trees. Several pieces of fruit were on the ground, and in an instant Diamanto surmised the children had been trying to gather oranges.

Another blast went off, and Elaine's calls for help grew louder. Diamanto, using all of her strength to will herself to remain calm, took a breath and hushed her daughter as she came closer to the tree. She forced a comforting look that she hoped would ease Elaine's panicking. Her daughter's legs and arms were wrapped around the tree's trunk, and her thin body was shaking.

"I had no idea. I'm so sorry, Mama," Elaine said, her voice trembling.

"We need to get you down. Slowly bring ..."

"I can't! I'm too scared," Elaine snapped back loudly.

Diamanto stood at the base of the tree, reaching, but she was too short to help her daughter down. When a third bomb exploded, the ground moved again. Elaine closed her eyes and gripped the trunk tighter, frozen to the tree. Kotso came out of the house hurriedly with a wooden chair. He held the base of the chair while Diamanto stepped up to retrieve Elaine. Slowly, she was able to get her down.

"I'm sorry. I'm sorry. I'm sorry." Elaine begged for forgiveness through muffled sobbing, her face buried in the embrace of her mother and grandfather. "I thought I could grab some oranges to eat. I was hungry."

Diamanto and Kotso brought her inside the kitchen, where they covered her cold body with a blanket. Georgia made apologies to the old couple for the commotion. When all the children had settled down, Diamanto returned them to the bedroom. She covered her children once more as Elaine's whimpering softened. Sitting on the floor beside the two older ones, she watched Maria fall asleep in the arms of Georgia.

Although she knew Elaine had good intentions, she would need to scold her daughter with conviction, she thought, explaining once again the role of an eldest child. She had to remind Elaine to set the proper example for George and Maria. But not today and perhaps not tomorrow. Elaine would never do that again, Diamanto realized as she rubbed the back of her daughter, thanking God she was out of danger.

George, still awake, turned over with a tearful face and asked, "Where do you think Baba is?"

Before she could answer, he added, "Do you think Grandfather is right? I heard him say that the war will end soon. Then maybe we can go back and live in our house and have our things back. Do you think so?" His face was full of desperate hope.

Elaine started crying again, and Diamanto knew he had unintentionally upset her.

"Someday soon," she answered. He started to ask more questions, but instead of letting him continue, Diamanto stroked his head and quietly sang her favorite hymn, sung to bless the loaves of sweet bread at the end of the Greek Orthodox liturgy. "Rich men have grown poor and gone hungry," she sang, "but they that seek the Lord shall not be deprived of any good thing."

As she made the sign of the cross and sung the children to sleep with devotions to God, she prayed for Tasso's safety, an end to the war, and their return to a normal life.

Chapter Fifteen

A quick, high-pitched noise startled Diamanto one afternoon as she rested beneath a large olive tree adjacent to her Magoula field. As the war continued, she felt like her peace of mind eroded more each day. Every strange sound made her jump.

"Did you hear that?" she asked, turning to her mother, who sat on a blanket beside her with the children. They were cracking walnuts. Georgia put down the bundle she held in her hands and looked up.

When the sound repeated, Diamanto looked farther down the road where the noise emanated from. She heard it again, like a whistle. Springing to her feet, she gathered the children and stood next to Georgia. Perplexed, she tried to assess the sound. A sort of shuffling grew louder. Her heart quickened as she peered down the road. When she saw a long procession approaching, her eyes grew wide. There was a Nazi in front of the group. She could see he was holding a gun.

"What is it, Mama?" asked George, pulling on her sleeve.

"Hush!" Elaine said to him, taking Maria's hand. Diamanto motioned to the children to stay quiet.

Leaving the blanket and food, she led the children and her mother toward the edge of the field, where they could look down the road from behind a group of larger trees and remain unseen. When they had settled into their hiding spot, she gave hushed warnings to the children to stay silent.

A German voice called out to the bodies that followed. A sluggish group appeared through the dust that kicked up from the dirt road. The men following the Nazi weren't wearing German uniforms. Absent was the synchronized movement of a well-trained unit. They were almost lethargic in pace. When they got closer, Diamanto gasped. Row after row of Greek prisoners walked with their heads down. Some limped. Many had bleeding cuts and bruises. Their clothing was torn and dirty. There were at least two dozen rows of them. Her mouth hung open when she realized some of them were locals. Mr. Manitis was at the end of the fifth row. She knew him immediately because he had walked with that recognizable limp since childhood. She also recognized Mr. Panos, Magoula's schoolmaster. His wife was from Vassara. He looked unhurt, but how had he ended up in enemy hands?

With a quickening heartbeat, she scanned the lines, looking for Tasso. Georgia seemed to be doing the same. As prisoners marched forward, Diamanto moved down toward the olive trees. Through the trunks and branches that skirted the property, they peered into the street at the horrific sight just a short distance away. She assessed there were about fifty paces of protective shrubbery to hide behind before the ground stood bare, and they would be exposed. While she still had the chance, she searched for Tasso.

Midway through the lines of men was a prisoner slumping along, taller than most. His head hung down like the others, but it was turned away from the orchards, so that she couldn't make out the front of his face. He appeared to be looking to the other side of the street. A cold sweat broke out over her body. She knew immediately it was Tasso.

Diamanto moved along the fence with speed, trying to remain parallel with the line of prisoners as they marched and keeping a constant eye on him. Was he hurt? If so, she knew he would want to disguise his height and remain unseen by his family. She pulled George along by the hand and nodded to Elaine, who was approximately twenty paces away, to keep an eye on Maria. Elaine nodded back in return. The girls stopped behind a tree trunk and squatted down at its base. Diamanto and George kept moving. Keeping stride along the fence, she heard the Nazi officer yell something at the men. Her eyes were fixed on Tasso as tears ran down her cheeks. She felt breathless.

Suddenly, Tasso brought his chin back to center, and as he did, George immediately called out, "Baba! Baba!" Diamanto bent down to cover her son's mouth with her hand, but the damage was done. When the Nazi whistle blew, and the men were stopped, she closed her eyes in despair. A

German officer held up his hand and called out. Three Nazi soldiers came running as he pointed toward them. Her heart sank.

The officer yelled something in German. He looked back and forth over the fields where they hid. She and the children didn't move, but then a soldier from inside her courtyard called out. The officer from the procession approached the gate of her house. Through the trees, Diamanto saw the soldiers sitting at her table. They got up and approached the other German. As they talked from either side of the closed gate, the officer on the outside passed a piece of paper through the iron railings. The soldiers took the paper and looked at it while Diamanto turned back to her family, realizing in sudden fear that Kotso was not with them. She scanned the orchard but didn't see him anywhere.

When she looked back at the courtyard, she noticed that the "cheese soldier," as the children had come to nickname him, was among the group at the gate. He read the piece of paper and pointed to the fields. Diamanto prayed he was explaining that her family had permission to work the land and that they were no threat. She hoped a simple explanation would cause them to move on. But what about Tasso? Where was he going? How had he been captured? Where in the world was her father?

Her eyes shifted from her husband, whose expression was full of despair, to the Germans officers speaking with one another, to the fields, where she looked for her father. Perhaps he had heard the Germans and fled to the opposite side of the property? No, she thought, he would never leave them, especially Georgia. Moments lingered for an eternity while an avalanche of thoughts ran through her head. The tone of the Nazis speaking at her gate grew more intense. There was shouting, and the cheese soldier yelled something curtly at the officer in the street. When she saw him hang his head down, she grew even more afraid.

Looking back at Tasso with tears streaming down her face, she saw he was crying too. A strong pain erupted in her stomach, as if her insides were collapsing. Tasso lifted his head and looked around, and she wondered if he was searching for her. Without caution, she stepped slightly to the left, out from behind the tree trunk where she had been hiding, hoping he might see her. She stood in the open only for a moment, with George holding her hand as he cried. When Tasso's eyes met hers, she saw his mouth fall open. She quickly went back again behind the tree but leaned out just enough for him to keep sight of her. She wanted to shout out the way George had but stopped herself only to protect the children.

Tasso half-grinned at her with softening eyes. She wiped her tears. Although no words were spoken, Diamanto sent him messages of love from her heart and felt him answer in return.

My darling.
My beloved.
How I have missed you.
You are beautiful.
I'm so sorry, Tasso.
My Mandini, stay strong.
You look thin, Tasso.
Don't be afraid for me, Diamanto.
What will happen to you?
I have no idea where they're taking us.
We wait for you.
I wait to hold you.
I fear for my father.
I fear for your father.
I love you.
I love you.

Their silent communication was as audible to her as if the words were spoken aloud. She wished she could stop time and remain in that moment forever. Gazing at him with longing, she felt him hang on to the view of her as well. This was the purity of their love, she thought to herself, perfect and mutually instinctual.

The peace was broken by another blow of the whistle from the German officer in the street. When Diamanto turned, she saw Kotso walking slowly in the field, carrying a bundle of branches. She watched him stop cold and realized he must have been away from the house, unaware of the commotion. If only he had returned a while later, she thought. Kotso looked around with a puzzled expression. Meanwhile, two soldiers headed into the field toward him. He hadn't moved, but one of the soldiers shot his gun up in the air, causing her to fall to her knees. Kotso dropped the branches and raised his arms in compliance. When the two Nazis reached him, they pulled down his arms and escorted him across the field. He went with them without a struggle.

Diamanto pulled her mother into her chest to muffle her cries. The children huddled close as they watched in fear. Kotso was added to the line of prisoners. Would they come for them now? Would they take the children too? She held her mother tightly as they all wept. Elaine held Maria close to her waist just as Diamanto embraced Georgia.

"No!" said George.

"Hush!" snapped Elaine. "Or they could take *us*!"

Tasso's head hung low as Kotso was placed in line. The German officer yelled out, and the shuffling began again at a slow, pathetic pace, the melancholy sound of captured men.

Trembling, Diamanto crumpled to the ground, holding her children and mother for a long while before she could rise. Her father was gone. Where were they going? What should she do now? Her worst fears took over her thoughts, and Diamanto worked hard to stop the fearful images that attacked her mind. Thankful they had left, she forced herself to concentrate on prayer and consoled the children. Georgia didn't speak. Nor did she offer her pain-concealing smile. Diamanto suddenly realized she was in charge and would have to keep everyone safe from now on.

After a long time weeping, Diamanto determined it would be best to return with her mother and children to Sparta. They gathered their bundles of vegetables harvested from the field that day. Elaine and George hadn't stopped whimpering.

"Why do they have Baba?" George kept asking.

"And what about Grandfather? He is too old to be a prisoner!" Elaine protested.

Diamanto couldn't begin to explain the complexities of their situation. She struggled to collect herself and answered, "We can't discuss this now. We need to leave Magoula."

"My Kotso!" Georgia moaned. As they walked slowly back to Sparta, she murmured her husband's name over and over.

Adding to their pain was the hot, late-afternoon sun burning overhead. Diamanto told the children and her mother that they would not return to Magoula for a few days. She was shaken and needed to figure out a next step.

As they reached the city, there were several groups of women standing together, on doorsteps and in front of the town's cathedral. Diamanto wondered whether they had seen the prisoners as well. She told her mother and the children to rest on a bench within the cathedral's courtyard while she approached the women.

"Excuse me. My name is Diamanto Stamatopoulos. I just saw my husband with a large group of captured men in Magoula. The Germans have taken my father too, and I wondered if you saw them come through town, or if you know anything." The words came out of Diamanto more calmly than she had anticipated. She looked at their weeping faces.

"All of them. They've taken all of them!" one old lady cried as she put a kerchief to her reddened face.

"They're going to Haidari, near Athens," another added.

Diamanto gasped and for a moment was speechless. "Haidari?" she asked after a pause, wondering whether the woman's information was valid, remembering details her father had told her of the dreaded political prison camp where Greeks, Jews, and even some Italians were held. Her knees felt weak once more.

Before she could inquire further, a third woman added curtly, "They will be killed there for sure!"

The shock of her comment struck Diamanto hard, and she grew angry in protest. How dare she speak so offensively! She resented the woman's ignorant audacity and couldn't help but snap back. "You don't know that!" she said and walked away. When she reached the bench, she noticed Georgia was worse.

"Let's get you back to the room, Mother. You look pale," she said, helping Georgia up from the bench.

"What did they say?" Elaine asked.

"Nothing. They don't know anything," she answered, pulling Maria up to her chest.

They did not stop again along the way to their room. Diamanto feared ignorant comments the children might hear from other people on the street. After they settled themselves in Sparta, and she told the landlords what had happened, they brought the family some dried figs and tea. Georgia was given a little wine and put to bed. Diamanto tried to comfort

Elaine and George, who were still distraught. She rubbed their heads while they sipped their tea and then brought them into the bedroom to sleep.

As they settled in, she said, "Your baba and grandfather will be all right. They will be given food and somewhere to sleep until this war is over," she told them.

"How long ago was Baba taken?" George asked.

"I don't know, George," Diamanto answered. "But they are part of a very large group, so that is a good thing. The Germans are probably just holding the Greek soldiers together until this war is over, which may be very soon. We have to pray and be patient and stay strong for your grandmother. Can you do that for me?" She looked at the children lovingly. Elaine nodded, her face wet with tears.

Although she doubted all of what she had told the children, she hoped some of her lies might be true.

She sat up in the bed, holding them tightly in her arms as they fell asleep stretched across the small mattress and across her lap. She leaned her head back against the hard, stone wall and closed her watering eyes.

For two days, Tasso tried to get the attention of the German soldier in charge of night watch. After stopping in the town of Tripoli overnight, the prisoners had been locked inside the Church of St. Basil. He wasn't sure why they remained there and wondered whether the Germans knew what to do with them. Meanwhile, his legs and lower back ached. They had walked the almost sixty kilometers from Sparta to Tripoli with few stops. Worried about his father-in-law, he focused his mind on the present, wondering what he could do to help the old man. But although he worked hard to distract himself from thinking about his wife and children, Tasso kept seeing Diamanto's face and the way she had looked at him before they were taken away. He worried as much for her state of mind as he did for her safety. Seeing Kotso taken away must have destroyed her, as he knew it must have crumbled Georgia. All he could do for his wife was look after her father.

"Are you in any pain?" he asked his father-in-law again.

"Please, there is nothing you can do for me," Kotso answered as they sat near each other on the hard, cold ground. Several elderly men hadn't made it to Tripoli. Tasso had seen several topple to their knees from exhaustion, and they were immediately shot. If anyone dared to help them, they were killed as well. Tasso was afraid that the horrors Kotso had seen had taken away any last bit of hope he had, and for two long days, the old man sat silent in the house of God.

Tasso got up repeatedly to peer out a small stone window, trying to assess who was in charge. The same German soldier remained on night watch both evenings. He seemed to understand a few basic words in Greek.

As the door was opened and a few buckets of water were set down with some dried bread, he said, "Please. Let him go," pointing to Kotso while the old man sat slumped over. "He is no threat to you," he added.

The German soldier looked at Tasso and then turned and locked the door. Tasso squatted down and put his arm around Kotso, trying to give him water.

Stripped of glittering valuables, the church was cold and bare. Only the painted icons on the walls adorned what otherwise would have been a beautiful sacred building. The altar's golden chalice had been removed, along with a large Bible covered in gold leaf. A faint smell of incense hung in the air from past liturgical services. Only a handful of candles remained lit because even candles were stolen by the Nazis. What broken wax stubs could be found glowed in a white stand, offering a somber light through the darkened church. Sitting at the foot of the altar, one Greek soldier held a small, leather-bound gospel that had been left behind. It had no value to the Germans. The soldier read from it aloud in low tones that carried through the somber, dim room. Tasso listened as his comrade offered prayers of memorial and words from the holy gospel.

To the left of the altar, another group of men sat underneath a large painted icon of the Virgin Mary, each of them staring up at Her with desperate pleas. Prisoners spread all over the floor and in corners of the room, all of them hungry and dehydrated. What few buckets of water were brought by the Nazis hardly provided enough nourishment. Younger, less injured men tended to the lame.

Some critically hurt soldiers had collapsed the day they arrived near the altar and remained there, seeming to await death. They whimpered themselves to sleep with prayers to God for salvation. Tasso looked around the church at his hopeless comrades with a heavy heart.

Later, the Nazi returned with two more buckets of water. Tasso tried again. "Please let him go," he said through the small stone window. "He is old. He will die. Keep me. He is not a soldier." He looked into the German's eyes. The soldier shut the door and turned away without a word.

The next morning, the third day of their captivity, Tasso was startled when the German approached the wall's opening. "Your father?" the German asked in broken Greek.

"Yes, yes," Tasso said, nodding energetically.

"Wait." The soldier said more, but "wait" was all that Tasso could understand. Still, he became elated with hope.

Tasso watched him walk farther into the darkness and then turned to Kotso. "Did you hear that?" he asked.

The old man didn't lift his eyes. Like the rest of them, Kotso appeared resigned to death. "You can't give up now! Diamanto and Georgia need you!" He placed both hands on Kotso's shoulders.

The old man's voice shook as he barely looked up to answer. "They need you too, Tasso. But I don't know if I can carry on. Perhaps it's God's will that I die here under the icons of Jesus and His holy Mother."

"No!" he answered back, pulling Kotso's shoulders toward him. "You will *not* die here! The women need you! You must go home and help our girls and George, no matter what happens to me!" As Tasso pleaded with him, all he could see in his father-in-law's eyes was despair.

"They'll shoot you if you anger them," Kotso answered. He finally raised his eyes to meet Tasso's. "Don't beg for me to be saved," he advised. "I've *lived* my life." He broke down in tears.

Tasso embraced him while holding back his own emotions. "Dear Kotso," he said, "you and the few elders in this church are the only Greeks with a chance. If they let you go, you must get to Magoula." Tasso held him for what he feared might be the last time.

The night grew colder, and Tasso waited anxiously for the German to return. Hoping he hadn't misread the Nazi's comment, he prayed there was a chance. He knew the older men were more frail than the younger soldiers, and the walk to Tripoli had made them most delicate.

There was a rumble of chains outside the church's door. Tasso sprang to his feet and immediately awakened Kotso. The old man barely opened his eyes as he lay on the floor.

White light from a waning moon created a ray of brightness through the doorway as it opened, with a shadowy figure standing on the other side. After a moment, Tasso recognized the Nazi who looked around the interior of the church and pointed his finger at various men. He seemed to be counting. Then he said something softly in German to a younger Nazi standing behind him.

The second soldier nodded and stepped forward. He spoke in almost perfect Greek. "You four older ones may go! Talk to no one. Do not look back, or we will shoot you!"

Tasso gasped aloud in happiness and disbelief. Turning to Kotso on the floor, he barely gave the old man a chance to stand up on his own. "Go!" he said as he lifted his father-in-law up and stood him upright beside the doorway. He turned around to make sure the others were coming forward. Three other old men wearily stood with the assistance of younger men.

As they moved toward the door, someone yelled out, "Tell Aspasia I love her! Tell her to kiss little Dimosteni for me."

Kotso put his hand on Tasso's shoulder. The old man's voice trembled as he looked in his eyes. "My Tasso, you couldn't have loved me more if you were my own son. No man was worthy of my Diamanto but you. Pray God you make it home to us. Thank you for what you have done." Kotso put his head down and slowly walked through the doorway with the other men, headed into the dark. The German slammed the door, and Tasso went to the window to watch the men leave.

When they were out of sight, he leaned on the side of the window and wept while whispering, "Thank you, Lord," over and over.

Chapter Sixteen

Nearly thirty minutes after they began walking, one of the men stumbled on a rock and nearly fell. Kotso reached out and caught his arm.

"Thank you," said the man. None of them had said a word until they were well past St. Basil's church.

"I'm Kotso," he said, looking up at the remnants of a waning moon that acted as their beacon.

"My name is Grigori. That's Prokopi, my brother, and my cousin, Saranto," the man said, pointing to the other two. They looked at Kotso and nodded.

"You're family?" asked Kotso.

"Yes," answered the man named Saranto. "Our sons are not as fortunate. Two of them are inside that church. Was that your son who saved us? I heard him call you 'Father.'"

Kotso choked up before he could speak, thinking about how he had resolved to die there. He would have too, if Tasso hadn't begged for his life. He was only partly grateful for his freedom; getting to Georgia and his daughter was his sole motivation. He fought back a tear before answering.

"My daughter's husband, yet no less a son from my own blood."

"Tasso, right? His name?" asked Grigori.

Kotso nodded.

"We pray God watches over them," Saranto added.

Then Kotso asked, "Why don't I know your family? I thought those men captured were from Magoula."

"We were coming to our relative's funeral from Kalamata. We knew the trip had risks, but one has to bury their dead. We were taken prisoner the same day as you," Grigori replied.

Another man added, "Word in Kalamata was that the hold against the Allies is weakening, that the war might end soon. Perhaps taking prisoners was a last act of desperation. All those men … something to bargain with."

"God keep them alive until peace is declared," Kotso answered.

"Amen!" added Prokopi.

A frigid breeze blew up the side of the hill where they walked, and Kotso estimated they were still many hours away from reaching Sparta. Without rations, he knew the long walk from Tripoli would be close to impossible, and he assumed the others understood the same. As he trembled, his sore limbs and aching back were nothing compared to the misery he felt mentally, unable to erase the faces of men shot to death. He gathered he would never be able to remove the painful images from his memory. After a while, the pain became more than he could bear. He found it hard to move.

"Should we stop?" he asked. "I know it's best if we keep going, but …"

"You're right," Grigori said immediately, as if he possibly had been thinking the same thing. "I'm guessing it's after midnight with the way the moon hangs in the sky. We can barely see a thing!"

They slowed their pace and looked around for a place to rest, heading off the side of the road to the brush. Kotso squinted his eyes at what he thought was a strange square shape ahead. Approaching it with reservation, he realized it was a *mandri*, a small stone structure where shepherds took shelter.

"Well, if it's good enough for a shepherd, it's good enough for us!" Grigori said.

They entered carefully, making sure it was empty since Greek resistance fighters were known for hiding out in the hills. This one seemed empty. Kotso bent over to accommodate the low-ceilinged doorway. The tiny hut was nothing more than a bare stone room where a man would rest while letting his goats or sheep graze on the mountainside. It made a tight fit for all four of them. Two small, square windows on either side of the room allowed air to come in. Kotso bumped into one of the men as he kicked his feet around the corners of the structure, looking for anything left behind. When something struck his foot, he bent over to feel a rough material.

"I think I've got something," he said. "Oh, it's a blanket."

"Good," replied Saranto.

"Do you think we'll be safe here?" Prokopi asked as Kotso opened the coarse woolen fabric on the floor.

"Better than stumbling through the dark!" answered Grigori.

Kotso felt around the other edges of the room, saying, "We should leave before the sun comes up." The back of his heel hit something hard that clanked across the floor. "Oh!" he said with excitement.

"What is it?" a voice asked.

He wasn't sure which one of them had inquired as he bent down to feel around at his feet. It was an oil lamp. "Light, my friends, light!" He picked up the lamp and bent down again. "I don't know if there are any matches, but …"

"Here!" Prokopi said. Kotso felt a hand on his arm and a small box put into his palm. "I took these from the church before we left," Prokopi admitted.

"What?" asked Saranto.

"Well, they were on the floor next to me by the altar, and when I found out we were leaving … God forgive me, but I grabbed them," he confessed.

"It's a blessing you *did*!" Kotso said, opening the box and striking a match. A soft glow illuminated the dark room. Kotso smiled as he looked at the faces of the men he could now distinguish in detail. They smiled at each other. He nodded back as if to reacquaint himself with them in the light.

"There's not much room here and only one blanket," Grigori said, "but to have light!"

"Yes," said Saranto. "We'll have to lie like we did when we were kids, right, Prokopi?" There was a laugh from the men.

Kotso lay on his back next to the three strangers, unable to sleep. As he stared out the hut's tiny window, it felt good to rest his legs and back. Georgia was on his mind. He worried about the women and children. *Diamanto carries the heaviest burden of her life*, he thought as he rubbed his forehead and closed his eyes in silent prayer.

Daybreak came only a few hours later, but the men were already on the move. "Alepohori—that's the town we should reach this morning, if my sense of direction is any good at all," Kotso said.

"Not far. We have a cousin there. It's our best chance for food and water," Saranto added.

Sparta was still many hours away, and he knew they needed water soon. After a little more than an hour, they found themselves on the outskirts of Alepohori. Even though they were close, Kotso was at his breaking point. He had to keep stopping, and so did Saranto.

"I'm sorry, men," Saranto said apologetically. "It's my bad knee. The pain has become more than I can bear. Perhaps you should go without me."

"Absolutely not!" Prokopi insisted.

"Maybe he's right," Kotso added. "I have to keep resting my back. Maybe the two of you should continue, and we'll catch up slowly."

Grigori came over to Kotso and sat on the ground next to him. "No. Separating would be a mistake." Prokopi nodded in agreement.

Kotso tried to catch his breath. Dizzy spells had been coming over him repeatedly, although he had said nothing to the others. After about twenty minutes, Grigori helped him up, and Prokopi assisted Saranto. The two stronger ones practically carried Kotso and Saranto until they reached the outskirts of Alepohori. They stopped near a well and a stone bench, where three little girls saw them and ran to help. A woman came toward them while another ran off, yelling that she would get others. "Quickly! Give them water!" someone said.

Within minutes, a priest arrived, trotting down the dirt path, his belly bouncing underneath his vestments.

"Are they hurt?" he asked the woman.

Kotso didn't have the strength to answer. Neither did the others.

"I don't think so. None are bleeding," said a woman who looked him up and down.

Kotso drank without lifting his head, but he could hear the commotion of many voices. Relatives of the other men arrived and began fussing over them. An older man brought him a piece of damp bread and cheese. Then the travelers were helped into a nearby home, where he rested on a couch. Women wiped his forehead with a damp cloth and offered a small pillow for the back of his head. Too weak to talk, he nodded in appreciation.

Watching the swirl of activity surrounding him, Kotso couldn't help thinking about the assistance he and his family had experienced in recent years. He reflected on Tasso's story of Niko and Christo and what Tasso had told him about Niko's wife Antonia. This is what it must have been like for Tasso in Elaiohori, he gathered. Even Petro came to mind for loaning Tasso his wagon when Nikola was ill. These were his countrymen, he concluded. *We are a good land made of good people, God-fearing and honest,* he thought. He wondered why some men turned on each other while others reached out with all they had. Ultimately, however, he knew that in some constant thread of hope, God had been with each of them in some way.

Kotso was moved to a room where he shared a bed with Saranto. Many hours later, he opened his eyes and noticed the sky outside was black. A small oil lamp was lit on a side table. He looked over and saw Saranto sleeping. Then he noticed a kind-looking girl with blonde hair sitting in a chair next to Saranto's side of the bed. She couldn't have been that much older than his granddaughter Elaine.

"Can I get you anything?" she whispered sweetly.

"Have I slept all day?" he asked, groggy.

"Yes," she said with a smile. "All of you have. It's nearly midnight. I just wanted to keep an eye on my uncle Saranto." There was a ragged doll in her lap.

"You remind me of my granddaughter," he said. "You are very kind." He tried to sit up but felt too weak. He lay back down and closed his eyes. "I think I'm going to rest more," he told her.

The following morning, Kotso awoke feeling much better. His dizziness had dissipated, and his back hurt less. After cleaning up, he joined the men at a small wooden table in the kitchen. The women moved about the room in a steady flow of activity, pouring, slicing, and moving dishes, creating a chorus of kitchen sounds he knew well. Kotso wondered whether they ever stopped working. Plates of dried figs with hardened bread were placed in front of the men, and they ate. It was then that Saranto asked Kotso to stay with him and his cousins. They had decided to remain in Alepohori for several days. But Kotso insisted on leaving.

"Are you sure?" Saranto asked as they passed a small dish of figs. An older woman dressed in black refilled Kotso's teacup.

"I must continue," he answered after taking another sip of his floral-smelling tea. The steam soothed his face with its warmth. "My daughter and wife must be wondering if I'm dead or alive. I can't let them think the worst."

"But are you strong yet? You haven't rested enough. Stay another day," said Grigori.

"I'm much better," he told them.

"What if something happens to you on the way to Magoula? What if you are taken again? What if you get lost?" Prokopi asked.

Kotso smiled at his new friend, trying to ease the obvious worry that took over Prokopi's face. "I will be careful. Like you, I've grown up in these hills. I'll find my way," he tried to assure him.

Prokopi and Saranto looked down into their teacups. Grigori reached for another piece of dried bread and dunked it into his cup. He held it there, soaking in the hot liquid, and then took a bite. He wiped his mouth with the back of his hand and answered, "We understand. But if you change your mind, or even if you start out and want to turn back, you know we welcome you here."

Kotso thanked them for their hospitality, adding, "We Greeks are strong. We would be even stronger if we held together." He paused. "My biggest fear is not the Nazis, even after all we've been through. From what I've seen, it's camaraderie that's missing. Greek turning on Greek, tipping off the Germans for money, joining bands of rebel groups to hide in the hills. I understand the desperation, but I don't see how they can turn on their brothers. What will happen to us *after* the Germans leave?"

"And they will leave … soon. Talk of the Allies gaining strength has been increasing for weeks," Saranto added.

"These political disputes are breaking us into pieces," Kotso said.

There was a strange silence at the table, and no one commented for a while. Grigori and Saranto looked down at their plates.

"What?" Kotso asked them.

"My son," Prokopi said. "He is one of these 'rebels' you talk about. He's been with a band of men hiding in the mountains for months. We haven't seen him in almost a year."

Kotso sank back in his chair, ashamed that he had offended the men who had taken him in. "I didn't mean …"

Prokopi shook his head. "Don't. I agree with most of what you say.

It's just that I've been on the other side of things too, watching my son get involved with the resistance movement. They really do want what's best for Greece, you know."

"May God bring us all together again in peace," Saranto added.

Kotso appreciated his effort to smooth things over but said, "Truly, Prokopi, if I've offended you, I apologize."

"You haven't, friend. We are *all* Greeks," he answered.

Shortly after breakfast, Kotso was packed up for his trip with bread, water, and dried fruits to get him through the rest of the journey. He had enough provisions even if his trip took longer than anticipated. After thanking his friends and their families, Kotso set out alone to reach Diamanto, Georgia, and the children.

Two days passed as he walked many hours to reach Sparta. He stopped only to rest briefly and to wait out the darkness. His back started to hurt again, and he almost passed out from exhaustion just a few houses down from the room the family rented in Sparta. Bracing himself against a tree, Kotso paused to catch his breath. An old woman came to offer help and recognized him. She told him to stay put while she rushed off for Diamanto and Georgia.

"Father!" called Diamanto when she came out of the house with her mother, Georgia following behind.

"Oh my Lord!" Georgia yelled. When his wife reached him, his body started to collapse on top of her. She kissed him all over his cheeks and forehead as Diamanto grabbed him to stop him from falling.

He let out a small moan because that hurt too. But he had never been so glad to see his wife and daughter. "Are you well?" he asked.

"Father! We are fine, but *you* are our concern! How did you get free?" Diamanto asked.

Before he could answer, his left leg slipped, and he almost fell. It was hard to straighten his limbs again, and he used the tree to lean on as the women took a hold of him on either side of his body.

"Where are the children?" asked Kotso.

"Helping our landlady with the laundry," Diamanto said.

"Good. I don't want them to see me like this," he replied.

"Let's get you inside," Diamanto instructed.

"Did they hurt you?" Georgia asked with her arm around his waist. Slowly she helped him move. As he took a step, every muscle ached. He could barely feel his legs. He shook his head.

"Go slowly. Here," Diamanto said as she went underneath her father's left arm. Together they shuffled him into the home, resting him on the living room couch. He sat down and looked up at both of them. Diamanto pulled up a chair for her mother.

"Tasso," he said. "He saved us. They let the elder men go because of him." He rested his head back on the couch as Georgia covered him with a blanket.

Diamanto started to cry, sitting at his feet with her arms on his lap. "He's alive?" she asked with eyes full of tears.

He lifted his head, eager to give good news. "Yes. Tasso is alive." He went on to tell them sparingly of their transport to St. Basil, leaving out ugly details. But he told them about Saranto, Grigori, and Prokopi and the increasing rumors about a possible end to the war. He knew they needed something positive to ponder, even if peace was still uncertain.

"We haven't been back to Magoula, Father," Diamanto told him. "We were too scared."

He reached out to take her hand. "Rightfully so, my dear. I also think it best that we remain here until we know what is happening."

After a while, when his back felt better, Georgia came to help him clean up, carrying a pail. She said little as she dipped a towel into warm water and washed his shoulders and arms gently. He stopped her and put the cloth down, holding her hand and leaning forward to touch his forehead to hers. Like a young bride, she melted into his wet chest and wept.

"I thought you were gone forever," she whispered.

Kotso pulled her close. He kissed her cheek and held her face, still seeing the beautiful girl who lived in her eyes, unchanged in their lifetime together. "Not yet," he answered. "You still have to take care of me for some time," he added, trying to make her laugh. She smiled, which made his heart happy.

Dressed in a clean shirt, Kotso entered the main room of the house just as the children burst through the door. Yelling out for their grandfather, they ran to him and threw their arms around his waist. He had never been so grateful to see their smiling faces. He sat with them in the kitchen as Georgia stood by his side and Diamanto brought coffee to the table. She set down a tray on the table and handed her father a cup.

"Thank you," he said to her before turning to the children, who were watching him with eager expressions. He wanted to dispel their fears and told them that their baba was alive and well.

"But why did they take *you*? How come Baba isn't with you?" George asked.

Kotso put his cup down. "Your baba is a tough man." He paused and then added, "And I believe this war is almost over."

Diamanto winked at him and told the children to save their inquiries until after their grandfather finished his tea and relaxed. Kotso wrapped his arms around all of the children as he sat on the kitchen chair. He had to keep putting his teacup down when George, Elaine, and Maria got up repeatedly from their chairs to hug him once more. It became like a game, and they laughed louder each time one of them went into his arms. He repeatedly pretended that he was about to lift his teacup off the saucer and raise it to his mouth again, but every time he did, George, Elaine, and Maria exchanged turns embracing him, laughing harder than before.

Chapter Seventeen

Like the cooler winds that marked a definite transition from summer to fall, there was a noticeable difference that evening. Aside from the absence of stifling heat and the presence of a welcome autumn breeze, Kotso was conscious of other changes: fewer explosions, fewer troops on city streets. Talk in the streets of liberation increased, and he clung to the optimistic idea of the war's end.

Less than a week later, as he sat at the kitchen table to keep his wife company while she washed dishes with their landlady, the quiet afternoon was interrupted by the clanging of church bells. Georgia put down her dishtowel and came to his side.

"What is that?" she asked with a concerned look.

Kotso's heart leapt. *At last*, he thought. "I think it's finally over!" he said.

Together with the landlady, they went to the front of the house and opened the door. People came out of their homes wearing the same eager expression. Some had tears streaming down their faces. Others shouted, "Peace!"

Diamanto came from the bedroom carrying Maria in her arms. "What is it? What's happened?" She held Maria tightly. "They are shouting, 'Peace!'" she said. "Is it over?"

He smiled at her. "Let it be so!"

Like the celebrations of Easter eve in the Greek Orthodox Church, when Jesus Christ's resurrection is commemorated with clanging bells at the strike of midnight, the same joy of renewed life rang out across the city. Crowds of people filled the streets, all cheering.

George and Elaine ran into the house from outside. "It's over!" they shouted in unison. Georgia and the landlady made the sign of the cross.

"Oh, thank God!" Diamanto said, bouncing Maria in her arms.

Kotso opened his arms to receive his wife, who put her head to his chest and embraced him.

He took everyone outside together to see what was happening, and a neighbor greeted him from across the street with a smile, handing over a glass of cherry brandy. They toasted to peace and embraced. Proceeding down the street, he saw everyone had the same idea and was headed into town. Churches along the way had their doors open, and large groups of people stood outside. Many of them held lit candles. When Kotso passed St. Nikonas, he sent his grandchildren inside to light their own.

As they proceeded to Sparta's town square, Kotso, although overjoyed, quietly wondered whether the euphoria would last. What of the resistance groups? What of the political instability? He scanned the area and looked at adjacent municipal buildings once occupied by the Germans and read the graffiti on the exterior walls. Although some of it featured messages such as "peace," other writing praised the guerilla actions of the *andartes.* As much as he wanted to celebrate international peace, he knew that internally, Greece's stability was far from settled.

"What is it, Father? Aren't you happy?" Diamanto asked as they stood surrounded by cheering Greeks.

"Oh, my sweet, I am," he said, wishing his emotions weren't always obvious to others.

"Is it Tasso you're worried about?" she asked.

"No," he answered. "Most likely, the Allies reached them without trouble. They'll be fine!"

"You look like something is wrong," Diamanto insisted.

"I'm just overwhelmed," he lied. She hugged him.

A few days later, the family decided to return to Magoula. Diamanto rose early, enthusiastic to see her home. She washed quickly and put on a dress and fixed her hair, all while wondering when she would see her husband. Had the prisoners been freed? When would he return? She was eager to see the status of her home and had no idea what they would find, but she longed to walk freely in her own courtyard. Her mind continued to ponder a thousand thoughts.

After helping Maria get dressed, Kotso appeared in the doorway. He wore a cautious look, the same expression as the day before. "I want you to be prepared today," he told her, "for whatever we find in Magoula." She didn't like his concern. "I don't want to cause you any distress," he continued, "but I'm doubtful the home will be in perfect shape."

"I know," she answered, trying to show her father that her expectations were realistic.

He took another step into the room and added, "Whatever happened to the house, rest assured, we can fix it over time."

"But you seem upset about other things," she said. "It's not just the house, is it?"

"No." Kotso paused. "There's still a good amount of unrest. I'm not sure if it will be safe for us to stay in Magoula, considering the guerilla groups. Lord knows they will be more active now than before," he warned.

Her smile evaporated, and she felt frustrated that her happy mood was being tempered. "I want to see Tasso," she told him. "I feel like once he is home, this nightmare will be over." She knew her answer sounded wishful, perhaps foolish. But hanging on to a vision of his return had sustained her all along, and she couldn't focus on another conflict. Caught somewhere between her mother's innocence and her father's precautions, Diamanto didn't want to be uninformed, but she wasn't sure that knowing all the details was a good idea either. She wanted Tasso. He would make it right and tell them what to do.

Later that morning when they approached the house, Diamanto noticed the large iron gates were open to the street. Her heart beat fast as she walked ahead with her father. Because of fear of what they might discover, the children were kept back and held hands with Georgia. She and her father approached with caution.

"Our house, Mama! Our house!" called out George. "When can we go upstairs?" All three children were jumping with eagerness.

Kotso turned and put his hand out. "Wait until your mama and I check it first, George. You have to be patient," he said. "Diamanto," Kotso said quietly to her, "walk about the place very carefully."

"I will," she agreed, inspecting the courtyard she had been forbidden to enter for so long. The small table where they had once eaten breakfast was turned over on its side. Chairs were thrown about the area as well. It looked to her as if a fight had broken out. There were pots of dirt turned over and broken glass. The walls of the exterior were undamaged, which her father said surprised him. As she looked inside the lower level through the cracked windows, the house seemed as sound as the day they had been removed. But she knew she would never again see the things taken away by the Germans.

Once inside the kitchen, she saw a plate left on the counter. She showed it to her father. He smiled back. She also found a few china cups and held on to them as she looked around more. Kotso said he would check the upstairs. Moments later, he called out that she could come up, so she put down her dishes and left the kitchen.

Running to her through the courtyard, Elaine asked, "Can I come upstairs too?"

"Not just yet, Elaine. Let me see what your grandfather wants." She quickly ascended the steps to the upstairs terrace. The balcony looked fine, although some of the glass from the front window had been broken. She stepped around it. Entering the home, she noticed that the map she had once seen on the wall from the outside had been removed. Scraps of paper were stuck to an empty nail. The corner where her shelf of icons had hung was bare, and she felt grateful to have saved the one.

As she walked about the upstairs floor, she looked into each room. More windows were broken, but she didn't care. She ignored the scratched walls and tried to stop thinking about the items that were missing. Whatever minimal pieces of furniture they had left behind were gone, except for the wardrobe. Diamanto was simply happy to be home again. But when she stepped into the bedroom, she was the most surprised.

"Father!" she yelled. "Look!" She pointed to the floor where there previously had been a hole to the downstairs. "The floor!"

Kotso covered his mouth with his hand. He bent down to feel the floor panels that reached the outer trim where Tasso had left off. The area once roped off for safety had been completed. "How strange!" he said.

"Why would they do this?" she asked.

"Perhaps there was a carpenter among them." Kotso half-laughed.

"Wait until Tasso sees this!" Diamanto added.

Kotso called to Georgia and the children, who came running upstairs. Maria ran across the new planks, oblivious to the fact that any ropes or gaping holes had been there.

"Wow! Who finished the floor?" George asked.

"The Germans?" asked Elaine.

"Baba won't believe this!" George said, echoing Diamanto's feelings. "When will he be back, Mama? The war is over. Where is he?" George tugged at her skirts.

She took a deep breath and bent down to open her arms to Maria. "It will take him a while to reach Magoula. The important thing is that we are here. This is the first place Baba will look for us."

Diamanto stood in front of the wardrobe, folding what few items of clothing they had—a few shirts, pants, and blankets they had kept with them—and placing everything neatly inside the bottom two drawers. With Maria playing contently on the floor with her doll, Diamanto matched the corners of a white sheet, folding it over her arm and smoothing out the fabric before putting it in its place. Her mind wandered as she looked inside the wardrobe. What was delaying Tasso's arrival? Ten long days had passed without his appearance.

It was as if Kotso was reading her mind when he entered the room. He gave her a sympathetic half smile, and she knew what he was about to say.

"We have to be patient, Diamanto. Tasso will return as soon as he is able." He put his arm around her.

She closed her eyes and shut the wardrobe's door, leaning against it. She couldn't reply. She was unable to find the words that could describe her anxiousness, her elation at the war's end but the worry she still harbored for her husband.

"We have to be smart," he added. "Trouble is breaking out on some of the islands, and Athens is no different. Men coming down from the mountains are in the cities now, and they will fight for control. The *andartes* are to be feared, Diamanto." He paused. "I'm afraid Tasso may not be done with this mess." He looked at her kindly. "I know that's not what you want to hear, but I have to tell you the truth. It's my job to protect you."

She was sad as she listened to her father. She loved him for his honesty, but at the same time, she felt enraged thinking of Greeks fighting Greeks. "I just can't understand that some of them are our very own people … these *andartes* … Some are from Vassara!" She looked at Maria sitting peacefully and wished her daughter could have her baba back.

"They are changed men," Kotso said. "They've become like animals."

"Do you think that's where Tasso is now?" She turned to him. "Fighting *them*?"

"I'm not sure. But stay strong in your faith," he advised. "I'm certain as soon as he *can* return, he will."

"It's been over a week!"

"I know." He embraced her.

She took a deep breath and told Maria to wash up for their midday meal. Then they went downstairs to help Georgia.

Later that night, she went to bed with petitions to God. She said the same prayer the following night and for another week after that, with still no sign of Tasso.

Chapter Eighteen

Tasso's heart beat faster as he neared Magoula, hoping the family was there. He hadn't thought of an alternate plan if the house was empty. It had taken him longer than he had anticipated, but he was so glad to be nearing home. His heart felt like it was bouncing inside his chest.

"Hello!" he shouted from the beginning of the dirt path, upon finally turning off the main road. A rooster simultaneously echoed a loud morning crow. No one answered. Finding the front gate locked, he cried louder than before. "Hello!"

A moment later, he heard the sound of happy screams, and an instant grin broke across his face. He exhaled in joyous relief.

"Baba!" he heard from the upstairs balcony. George, Elaine, and Maria descended the stairs in a rush. Elaine unlocked the gate and reached him first, and behind the children, Tasso saw his wife and in-laws running across the courtyard. The children encircled him, the two older ones clinging to his torso tightly while Maria held onto his leg. Her tiny arms squeezed his thigh tightly.

"Oh, you are beautiful! All of you!" he laughed, studying their gorgeous faces, each of them more lovely than he remembered. Diamanto had the widest smile he had ever seen.

"My Tasso!" she cried before he kissed her. She clung to his side and didn't let go. He tried to step forward into the courtyard and laughed; he had to use all of his strength to move his body with his children attached to him. George was practically pulling him down. He squatted down to scoop up Maria and held her on his hip as he embraced everyone. Kotso and Georgia's faces were glowing. He was so glad to see the old man had made it home.

"My boy!" Kotso said with outstretched arms. Tasso could tell from looking at him that his father-in-law was in much better shape. Overcome with relief, he didn't hold back the tears when they embraced.

"Thank you for what you did," Kotso said to him. Tasso nodded.

Diamanto put her arms around both of them and said, "I'm so happy to have you together! Come! Let's get you some food. Are you well? You're filthy!"

He swallowed hard and nodded, taking a deep breath. "So good to be home."

After Tasso had eaten, washed, and changed clothes, he sat inside their bedroom with his leg up on the mattress, inspecting the limb. But when he heard his wife's footsteps, he sat up quickly and pulled his pant leg down.

"Tasso?" she said as she entered the room.

"Is that for me?" he asked, looking at the tray with a small demitasse cup and saucer.

She nodded. "I thought I saw you limping earlier. You're in pain, aren't you?"

He looked down at his leg and then back at her, feeling defeated by the truth. "It started in Tripoli, but it's the least of my worries. I'll be fine," he told her, hoping she wouldn't fret.

She sat next to him on the bed and held onto him in silence. He closed his eyes and inhaled the soft floral fragrance of her hair, still in disbelief that he was home, with her, in Magoula. After all he had been through, his presence with all of them still seemed unreal.

He knew he would never share the details of what had happened to him with his family. He planned to tell them that he would explain everything later, hoping they would get distracted or forget or just leave it alone. He could never tell them the horrors of the men who had died at his side before the Germans finally left, or how the British forces had come to set them free. They didn't need to know about the soldiers who had bled to death and the sickly ones who had never made it out of the church. A reinjured leg seemed trivial after all he had seen.

As they sat there, he looked around the room, recalling what Diamanto had told him earlier about their house, the Germans, and her father being thrown down the stairs. He wondered whether there were details she was sparing him as well. Although it was hard to repress anger, Tasso wanted to focus on the joy of being home, even though he still had other adversaries to think about.

He closed his eyes as a disturbing memory flashed in his head, the image of his comrade shot while standing beside him when the Nazis marched them out of Sparta. He had yet to understand what it was God had laid out for him, but at every turn, there seemed to be another battle to fight.

"What will happen now?" Diamanto asked.

He exhaled, wishing he had a happy reply. "I will have to help defend the city, I believe. If these bands keep coming down from the mountains where they've been hiding all these months, I'll have no choice."

"But you've only just arrived!" she said, pulling out of their embrace. Her face was full of worry.

"I know," he said with regret.

The following week, Diamanto watched her husband and son as they sat at the courtyard table. Tasso was showing George the design he had made for their property, explaining how he had worked out the exact number of lemon and oranges trees they needed to acquire. She listened, assuming the orchard would endure further delay. Nevertheless, she was glad to see Tasso talking about the plans, giving everyone something to look forward to.

"So how many in all, Baba?" she overheard George ask Tasso.

"Three hundred fifty!" he answered.

George smiled widely. "That's a lot of trees!" the boy said.

Within the hour, there was a call at the gate. Peering over the balcony railing, Diamanto sensed trouble. A man she knew as Ronakos greeted Tasso. She watched as Tasso got up but did not invite him in. Instead, they stood facing one another on opposite sides of the iron railings. Mr. Ronakos's greasy hair stretched across his head horizontally—a poor attempt to cover a balding head, she thought. His eyes were beady too, and she noticed he wasn't looking Tasso in the eye. They spoke too quietly for her to hear the conversation, but her concern was confirmed when Tasso turned and asked George to go inside.

She didn't like the so-called Greek doctor from Magoula, rumored to sympathize with the Nazis because of his medical training in Germany years ago. Word in town was that his formal education was a lie. Was he a doctor, or wasn't he? No one knew Ronakos's real story. The "German-loving" doctor, too old to fight yet quick-minded enough to make self-serving arrangements with the enemy, was no friend to the Greeks, everyone had been warned.

Without any appearance of hardship, Mr. Ronakos stood erect in his gray suit, matching vest, starched shirt, and shiny shoes. *How does he have money to dress like that?* she wondered, thinking of everyone else in old clothing covered with patches, still fighting to put bread on the table. And his shoes! Most people had one pair, scuffed, with holes, she thought, looking down at Mr. Ronakos's polished, fine leather footwear. Her heart began to beat faster, and she felt her eyes squinting at the man she had always regarded as evil.

Watching Tasso tower over him at the front gate, she hoped her husband would send him away. Straining to hear their conversation, she couldn't make out a word. When Ronakos finally left, Tasso came up the balcony stairs toward her, his footsteps heavy.

"What did *he* want?" she asked.

There was a pause before he answered her. "Me," he replied, looking at her.

"No!" she said as she fell into his embrace.

"I know," he told her softly. "I know."

Tasso didn't talk about Ronakos for the rest of the day, but Diamanto felt like the unwanted man was still in their home for the remainder of the night. She couldn't shake his eerie presence, and she could tell Tasso was somewhere else in his thoughts.

When the sun rose the next day, Tasso was already awake and sitting in the courtyard, with his drawings for the orchard resting facedown on the table in front of him. Fearing Mr. Ronakos's return at any time, he wanted to wait for the man, whom he could no longer delay. It wasn't worth upsetting Diamanto more, he thought, so he hoped to handle the doctor's threats on his own, before they spun out of control. But he knew leaving again was inevitable. Recalling his conversation with the doctor, his answer echoed in his mind: "I will join you as soon as I am able, Ronakos." He had hoped to put the man off for a while. "My leg has become infected again. I would be of no use to you in my current state." For the first time he felt grateful for his injury.

"I have injuries too," Mr. Ronakos had answered. "And yet I'm still here, working for our country. We need you to help us save Greece, Tasso. Let's not forget what happened to your brother, Dimitri. His disappearance still eats at you, I'm sure." Tasso's insides burned with the thought. "And I'm sure it hasn't been easy for you to wonder what happened. Most likely you'll never see him again."

The man's disturbing words played over and over in Tasso's mind as he sat in the quiet of the courtyard.

With the briskness of the previous night still chilling the early morning air, a slight fog hung over the property, waiting for the warmth of day. Despite his troubles, a peace seemed to surround the area as he sat at the table alone. Tasso looked up at the home he had built, a million thoughts flitting around in his mind—flashbacks to the day he had begun construction, dreams he'd had of his home while trying to reach Vassara after Albania, horrors he imagined of Nazis taking the place for their own use. His house, like him, had been through great trials. Yet both had persevered. Somehow, both he and the house were still standing—he and his home, one and the same. The strong, thick walls of mortar held up so much more for his family than a place to live. The home was their victory, no matter what else befell them. They had survived.

This house, he thought, supported their future, which he regarded with optimism, knowing the children would run free in these fields and someday collect fruit from their trees. He was certain their future rested in these rooms, within the walls he had erected. His family would continue, he realized, with or without him. The Magoula house would not fall for anyone or anything. God had blessed him with that.

Suddenly, Nikola came to his mind, and he smiled for a moment, hoping he and Luka were well and would stay a part of each other's lives after the war. Keeping Luka with Maria in Vassara had been the right decision, he knew, and he imagined how happy the boys would be to celebrate the war's end, but sad to bid farewell to one another. Luka,

Nikola, the house, Kotso's rescue from the church—suddenly, it all started to make sense. Saving himself hadn't been the point after all. Whom he could save in the process was the real essence of his survival. A lump of emotion came to his throat, and his chest swelled up, as he thought of the lives he had touched while his life had been spared. Father Tomas was right: God had a plan for him.

Tasso rose from his chair and went upstairs to the balcony, opening the door softly so as not to wake the children. He stopped for a moment in the hallway near the bedrooms where they slept. He looked at George's long body under the blanket, thankful the boy was too young to be a soldier. Knowing the seeds of a carpenter had been planted, he relished the idea that someday George might continue the same line of work. Taking a few soft steps to the second bedroom, he saw Elaine and Maria together under the sheet, eyes closed like angels. He smiled at Elaine's competent yet willful spirit and at his beautiful little Maria with long, curly black locks of hair, no longer a baby, soon ready for schooling. This was their Greece. What would become of it if he didn't hold back the *andartes* and keep the country safe for their sake?

An hour after sunrise, Diamanto awoke to voices in her courtyard. She rose and walked to the window, where she saw the dreaded Ronakos standing inside the gate, talking to Tasso. Again, they were speaking in low tones. She felt her knees go weak. Resigned to remain upstairs until he left, she washed her face, combed her hair, and got dressed while Georgia and the children were still asleep. Her father Kotso, however, was already up and gone. Diamanto assumed he must have walked into town early. He had made the trip every morning since the war ended, still seeking friends and cousins, trying to learn of losses and survival from townspeople in Sparta's main square.

When she heard the gate close, she paused for a moment before going downstairs to find her husband. Taking a deep breath, she held on to the railing of the balcony, knowing that she was about to learn of her husband's departure.

He was standing near the fence, looking at their cleared orchard fields when she touched the bottom stair. She could tell from the side of his profile that a troubled look spread across his face. Biting her bottom lip so as not to cry, she walked over to him, trying her best to maintain composure. She placed her hand gently on his back. When he didn't turn around to face her right away, she had her answer. He lifted his arm off of the fence and placed it around her shoulder, saying nothing. She stood there with him in silence for a moment, looking out onto the empty fields that awaited orange and lemon trees. There were few words to speak. The pain was palpable.

Finally, she asked, "When?"

"Day after tomorrow." His voice cracked.

"Where?" She swallowed hard.

"In the mountains. Near Taygetos." He cleared his throat. She knew he was trying to mask his own heartbreak.

"Perhaps then …"

"Of course," Tasso said before she could finish.

She smiled.

"They need me mostly at night. I hope to come back during daytime hours, between shifts. But I don't know when. I'll have to see how bad it gets. Mr. Ronakos says—"

"Mr. Ronakos is the devil himself!" she blurted, unable to hide her disgust for the man, even if she understood the cause.

"I don't want to leave, trust me, but I have to. Our country is in jeopardy, worse than before." He turned to her and put his hand upon her face. "You've been amazing. I know you can hold on a bit longer." He looked at her with adoring eyes.

She closed her eyes and pressed her hand against his where it rested on her cheek. "Oh, Tasso. I love you so much," she whispered. "And I know it's not about Ronakos. You do this for our children. You do this for your country." She paused and looked at him earnestly. "Please don't think I don't understand."

"I know you do. And I love you more than ever." He kissed her then and embraced her tightly, whispering, "We want bright futures for the children. They deserve to have a good life."

She finally let herself cry as she soaked in the feel of Tasso's warm embrace, holding in the sensation for memory. She nodded with a wet face, tears streaming down her cheeks.

Her father came through the gate moments later, looking anxious. He said he had to speak to Tasso right away. The two men headed into the orchard. She went to the kitchen to prepare something to eat, deciding to slice some cheese and fruit. As she placed a few pieces of cheese on a plate, she paused, thinking of Elaine, George, and Maria. Once again they would be without their baba.

Taking a deep breath, she sliced some dried figs while thinking of the days ahead and dreading the questions the children would ask, as well as the explanations she would be forced to make. The war had made her a soldier too, she thought, a soldier for her children, fighting to keep them safe and well. She put down her knife and lifted her eyes to the heavens, saying aloud, "Please, holy Virgin Mary, keep this country safe. Send down your blessings to protect these men, and once more, send my Tasso home in peace." She made the sign of the cross and stood there for a while with her eyes closed.

When she came out of the kitchen and returned to the courtyard, Tasso was sitting in a chair at the table with the three children around him. As he spoke, Diamanto noticed that Elaine was crying. George had watery eyes too. Her heart broke to see them learning of their baba's departure once more. She took another deep breath, confident she would teach them to be strong, just like Tasso had taught her.

Chapter Nineteen

Tasso prepared to leave two days later. Loading up a small sack, he kept his mind on the task ahead instead of on sorrow. This would be a far different fight, he thought as he rechecked the bag's contents, careful to bring only necessities. He expected to move often. After closing his satchel on top of the bed, he carried it to the top of the balcony stairs and set it down.

In the upper hallway, he stopped where their icon shelf used to hang. In its place was the icon that had belonged to Kotso, the one Diamanto had saved. It hung on a single nail and appeared odd by itself. He looked at the painted faces at the top: Jesus Christ holding the scriptures, the Virgin Mary, and St. John the Baptist. The lower section of the icon depicted St. George, protector of soldiers; St. Basil, caregiver to the poor; and St. Nicholas, patron saint of children. Angelic halos surrounded their heads, and their faces were painted as kind, portraying reverent expressions of devotion and purpose. He made the sign of the cross before calling out for Diamanto. She came quickly to his side, where he reached for her hand. They knelt together silently in front of the icon. Tasso bowed his head and closed his eyes, asking for peace, health, and safety. He heard Diamanto sniffle a few times while kneeling next to him.

When they concluded their prayers, he helped her up and said, "When I get back, I'm gong to build a new corner shelf for our icons." She smiled.

Descending the stairs hand in hand with his wife, Tasso was glad he had spoken with Kotso privately the day before. He felt confident that his in-laws understood the predicament with the *andartes*, and they had promised to stay in Magoula as long as it was safe. The actions of the guerilla groups would be hard to predict, but Tasso knew Kotso and

Diamanto could make good decisions together. Diamanto had proven herself to be strong, even if she was the last one to realize her own potential, he thought. After all she had been through, he knew she could hold on just a bit longer.

At the bottom of the stairs, he saw that his children wore glum expressions as they stood near the gate with their grandparents. They came toward him, and he could tell both George and Elaine had been crying. He took his daughter by the hand and pulled her close as George and Maria stood near.

Speaking softly, he said, "Elaine, you're in charge now. As the eldest, you have to help Mama to mind after your sister Maria, and remember to do as you're told."

"Yes, Baba," she answered. He hugged her tightly, kissing her atop the head through her beautiful hair. She picked up her head so that she could look at him. He smiled at her, and she returned a grin that he knew she was forcing with all her might. "You are a lovely young woman, Elaine. You light up this world, and I love you so much!" He fought back his own tears as he kissed her one more time before calling George over.

Tasso squatted down so that he and George were eye to eye. His words to his son about obeying Diamanto were similar, as he explained that George was now the second man in the house and needed to help Kotso protect the family. "I love you, and I'm counting on you," he told George as he held the boy for a long time. George refused to let go and then burst out wailing.

Elaine came to comfort her brother. "Come, George," she said.

When Maria came to kiss her father, she jumped into his arms playfully. He picked her up and hugged her, swaying her back and forth. His baby, he thought, the one who unmistakably held his image. He just had to come back to see who she would become.

"I love you, Baba!" she said to him, squeezing his cheeks together with her hands.

"I love you with all of my heart," he said to her, putting Maria down and turning to his in-laws. He embraced Georgia and Kotso.

"God be with you, son," Georgia said quietly.

"Be well, my son," added Kotso.

Taking Diamanto's hand, he led her away alone. "God will provide for them, Diamanto. I am certain." He knew his words weren't making this easier, but he needed to say what was in his heart. "Remember how we prayed. You will always be in my prayers, whether I am next to you or not. I will forever ask God to protect you and pray the Virgin Mary provides comfort through whatever challenges you face." He lifted her chin. "Try to find strength knowing this."

He pulled her close, inhaling deeply the beauty, goodness, and purity of his dear Mandini. From the day he met her in the olive field, she had been a part of him in every sense, and separating from her was the most painful. He kissed her lips and held her. Then, wiping away her tears, he smiled into her beautiful, sad eyes and told her he loved her. He waved to his in-laws and children one final time and headed up the road alone.

In the early hours of the morning three weeks later, Elaine sat upstairs in front of the fireplace while George and Maria played with a small ball in the same room. When she heard her mama shout, she looked at George, and together they darted out the door.

"Come, Maria!" Elaine told her little sister.

From the top of the balcony, she saw her mama embracing her baba. He had lifted her up to kiss him, and her feet were above the ground. Her grandparents stood close by, smiling.

"Baba!" Elaine yelled with the others, running down the staircase.

"Look at you!" he cried as he hugged them all together as one.

Elaine felt a tight squeeze as George and Maria were pressed to her sides within her baba's arms. She didn't mind the pain.

"Is it over?" George asked. "Are you home forever now?"

"No. But I have the morning and afternoon to be with you. I have to return to Taygetos before sunset to guard the city." He looked up at her mama and grandfather and added, "I am helping to protect the city at night, so I have to be back up there before dark." They nodded to him. Her mama was smiling like Elaine hadn't seen in a long time.

"You're filthy!" her mama said to him, shaking her head.

He laughed. "I know. Let me wash up. Do we have anything to eat? I'm starving!"

"I'll fix you something right away," said Georgia as she rushed off to the kitchen.

Elaine waited impatiently while her mama tended to her baba, bringing him clean clothes and soap. He went behind the house with folded items, saying he was eager to wash the many layers of dirt and grime from his body. Maria giggled. When he emerged, he looked like himself again, and this made her happy. He came to the table in the courtyard and sat. Elaine and her brother immediately went to his side. Maria sat on his lap.

"Are you hurt?" George asked.

"Just sore," he answered, smiling at them.

"Why don't we save our questions, and you can sit with Baba while he eats," their mama suggested.

Elaine wished she could ask him many things, but she knew with her siblings there, Baba wouldn't want to say anything to upset them. She stayed next to him while he devoured everything put in front of him. After a while, George and Maria began a game of tag in the courtyard, but she didn't want to play. She just wanted to be close to Baba, especially since he had to leave at the end of the day.

He looked tired to her, and she wondered what he had seen and where he had been. Where was he sleeping? Was he outside in the mountains all the time? Did he have to kill anyone?

When George tried to tag him while he was drinking his coffee, she got irritated. "Leave him alone, George. He's tired!"

But Baba got up and pretended to go after George. Maria let out a squeal, and within seconds he was chasing both of them. Elaine laughed and sprang out of her chair to join in the fun.

"Grab Baba's legs, but watch the bad knee, George!" Elaine shouted, trying with all her strength to pull him down with her brother's help. Her mama was laughing, and her grandparents yelled at them from the table to be gentle. He got loose from their grip a few times and pretended to run away, but Elaine could tell he was letting them catch him on purpose. Together in one clump of an embrace, they came down to the ground on top of their baba. She helped her brother and sister tickle him all over his body. He laughed and laughed and closed his eyes tightly. Maria climbed on top of Baba's chest and sat down, leaning over his face, where she tried with her fingers to open his eyes. Elaine laughed hysterically, watching them.

"You'll never do it!" Baba told Maria, twisting his head back and forth from side to side. But her tiny hands were all over his face.

"Oh yes, we will!" said George, who came to help Maria. It took all three of them to hold down his enormous body. But when he started to tickle her, Elaine had to give up, and all of them scattered.

Hours later, as afternoon ended, she was sad Baba had to leave. But he promised that before the week ended, he'd visit again for an afternoon, even if it was only a few hours. He'd try his best, he said.

"We love you!" she said as she waved to him with George and Maria. Their mama wasn't crying this time, and that made Elaine happy.

"I like these visits!" George said to her.

"Yeah. Can't wait to see him next time. For sure we'll win the tickle fight then!" she said.

"For sure!" George answered.

Nine days later, Diamanto was stripping the sheets off the mattress in the upstairs bedroom when she heard her children call from the courtyard that Kotso was home. He had gone up the road to visit an ailing friend and had planned to light a candle at St. Demetrios Church, but he wasn't expected back until later. She went to the foyer and saw her father coming through the balcony door with his head down. Kotso's face was without color, and his eyes were glassy. He walked hunched over, as if in physical pain. She thought for a moment he was hurt. When he asked the children to go downstairs, she knew something was wrong but wondered why he wasn't looking her in the eye. He led her by the hand back into the bedroom and told her to sit on the bed.

The source of his solemn demeanor came to her in one sudden, horrifying moment of grief. In a rush of melancholy, Diamanto let out an audible moan, burying her head in her father's chest. "No, no, no!" she wailed into his chest. "Not my Tasso. Not my Tasso!"

"Oh my dear, I'm so sorry!" Kotso cried to her. He held her tightly as wave upon wave of despair flowed over her body. The tragic realization hit her mind, then her heart, and then her soul and finally set in like a disease all over her delicate body. She collapsed like a child in her father's embrace, unable to move, unable to breathe. Anguish attacked her senses.

Kotso spoke to her through tears as he rocked her back and forth. "I hate that you've heard this news from me."

She was speechless for a long time and could barely find the strength to ask him what had happened. In so many ways, it didn't matter. He was gone, and nothing was going to make him walk through the gate again. The children quickly came up the stairs with Georgia when they heard her crying loudly. She couldn't look at their innocent faces as they were all about to learn the ill fate of their beloved father.

Kotso held her hands and explained, "When I went to visit my sick friend today, a boy was there. He was my friend's nephew." She looked at him as he struggled to speak.

"Tasso's group of loyalists was in the mountains near Mistras. They were guarding the city like he told us, trying to keep the rebels from entering Sparta and looting the city. They were ambushed in the middle of the night. The loyalists fought back and exchanged gunfire briefly, but they were surrounded and quickly outnumbered." Kotso's voice was shaking. He paused and looked first at his daughter as he held her hands and then at the children. She nodded for him to continue.

He struggled to get out the words but finally said, "Without mercy, they killed all but one who got away and ran into the darkness, saving himself. He reached Magoula and told everyone what had happened. The man is our neighbor's nephew." He broke down, taking Diamanto's hands to his chest as he wept. "This is all I know."

Anger began building inside her as she contemplated Tasso's murder. Hate and pain flowed into her mind. But in resigned defeat, she exhaled deeply and could only sense sorrow and emptiness. With the children wailing at her side, she held them tightly and wept for a long time.

A cold chill came over her body, as if she had been touched by something. She struggled to stand up, her legs shaking. She kissed each child's head. Remembering Tasso's promise of prayer, she walked over to the hand-painted icon where they had prayed together. She knelt down on the floor, made the sign of the cross, and said a prayer aloud for Tasso's soul. She asked that the Mother of God take him to Heaven by the hand

and welcome him to Paradise. The children followed her and knelt down beside her in like manner.

When she stood to come back to her father's side, she collapsed just short of the bed, her legs giving out underneath her. Crumpling to the floor, she leaned her head on her father's knees and cried. In the muted background of her mind, Diamanto overheard Kotso comforting the children. They sat on the floor with her, wailing as she held them tightly, pulling each of them close to her body, as if she was reaching for Tasso.

Diamanto remained there, next to the fireplace, for days, unable to function. Her mother offered soup brought to them by a neighbor, but she refused to eat. All sense of time and place was distorted as the hours and days melted into mournful grieving. She felt numb, unable to process any thought beyond the irony that her beloved Tasso, who had survived the battle at the Albanian border, who had been rescued from a sinking battleship, who had returned to Vassara first from the front lines, who had been taken prisoner by the Germans, who had negotiated the release of Kotso and the elders, and who had managed to build his family their dream home, lay dead at the hand of a fellow Greek. The atrocity was too much for her to bear, the injustice too large to measure.

Epilogue

Elaine squinted up toward the sun that shone brightly over the chaotic scurrying of passengers boarding the *SS New Greece* bound for New York. Although the sky was bright, Elaine noticed her mama's eyes had been clouded for days, perhaps longer. Even though Baba had been gone for several years, she rarely saw her mama smile. Their otherwise exciting trip to their country's capital had been washed over with solemn temperament and a desperate plea of hope. Now fourteen, Elaine understood the severity of their predicament, far better than her eleven-year-old little sister.

With all of their belongings packed into a single small brown suitcase, Elaine held their first-class passage tickets to America in one hand and Maria's palm in the other. Wearing her best outfit, a short-sleeved red dress, she made sure to put on a brave face for both Maria and her mama, clinging to the promise that a lovely cousin awaited them in New York, where they would be put on an airplane to a place called Montana, where their mama's sister Pota lived.

Her mama had promised to join them with George as soon as she saved enough money. Looking down at Maria, Elaine offered a false smile to reassure her that everything was going to be wonderful. Remembering Baba's words, she willingly took on the responsibility for Maria's happiness, feeling determined to ensure them a good life. With the tickets in her hand, she pressed her fingertips on the cross around her neck and said a prayer for strength as she watched Maria clutch her raggedy doll, a last item of their tragic childhood to carry into an unknown world.

"Mind your Aunt Pota, girls." Diamanto's face was covered in tears. Elaine kept her emotions inside as best she could, hoping her brave face would help her sister and their mama through a difficult farewell.

"Yes, Mama," she replied in unison with Maria.

"And Maria, stay close to your sister at all times."

"Yes, Mama," Maria answered.

Their mama kissed their foreheads, and they embraced together for a long time, until a man in uniform announced that the ship was preparing for departure. Elaine looked at their mama's sad face once more as she kissed Elaine on both cheeks. Bending down, Elaine picked up the handle of their suitcase with one hand and took Maria's hand with the other. Together they walked onto the ship, looking back several times at their mama.

After boarding the large vessel, Elaine made a place for them along the crowded, tall, thick railing on deck. They looked out to the port below and waved down to Diamanto, who was holding a white kerchief in her hand, which contrasted against the black of her mourning attire. The white kerchief moved up and down in the wind and seemed to wave Elaine and her sister on to their new lives, away from their mama, brother, and grandparents, away from the country that had taken Baba, away from the only home they had ever known.

But along with their homeland and family, Elaine understood they were also leaving behind death, hunger, and despair. The black was their tragic past, and the white, their promise of tomorrow, bright with hope and possibility. As the boat pulled away, the sight of their mama's black dress faded into the distance with the white kerchief flashing. Elaine and Maria's journey was just beginning.

Edwards Brothers Malloy
Oxnard, CA USA
January 25, 2016